Janey's Summer

MARY HOOPER

Illustrated by Paul Dowling

Janey's first summer job as a Robin at Robinson's Holiday Camp; it was going to be hard work but there'd be consolations ... Over six weeks at Robinson's – that meant six and a bit holiday romances. If nothing went wrong, that is!

Also by Mary Hooper

Cassie
Janey's Diary

the 'School Friends' series

First Term
Star
Park Wood On Ice
The Boys Next Door

MARY HOOPER

Janey's Summer

Teens · Mandarin

First published in Great Britain 1987
by Methuen Children's Books Ltd
Published 1992 by Teens · Mandarin
an imprint of Mandarin Paperbacks
Michelin House, 81 Fulham Road, London SW3 6RB
Reprinted 1992

Mandarin is an imprint of Reed Consumer Books Ltd

Text copyright © 1987 Mary Hooper
Illustrations copyright © 1987 Paul Dowling

ISBN 0 7497 1199 X

A CIP catalogue record for this title
is available from the British Library

Printed in Great Britain
by Cox & Wyman Ltd, Reading, Berkshire

Friday, 18th July

The house is in uproar. Mum is rushing around waving underwear at me and saying: 'You're not taking this awful *grey* thing, are you?' Jimmy is racing about behind her snapping at her ankles and Dad keeps bellowing: 'Oh, I do like to be beside the seaside!' very loudly and untunefully.

I've crept away to my bedroom to start this; I think it will be good to have it to look back on. Feel a bit jittery and squeamish about going away from home for such a long time – six weeks or so – but there's nothing else to do all summer; everyone else has got holiday jobs and James is on a six-month language course in Germany.

So, I'm running away to sea and I'm going to be a Robin hostess at Robinson's Holiday Camp at Burnham-on-Sea. I went for the interview last month and they explained to me what my duties would be: just keeping something like a thousand people happy from dawn until midnight, that's all.

'A Robin's prime duty is to see that the every need of our guests is attended to,' the personnel manager beamed at me. 'We're looking for staff who understand this.'

I beamed back and tried to make my expression dependable, helpful, loving and fun all at the same time. Difficult one, that.

'If you are chosen you can rest assured that we believe you to be the best person for the job. You'll have to be prepared to put in a lot of hard work. We don't want any shirkers.'

'Certainly not,' I said sternly, trying to look hardworking as well.

Two weeks later I got the letter saying they wanted me, and I start tomorrow. The wages aren't brilliant, but I'll be living in a chalet in the camp and getting all my meals, so what I collect will just be pocket money. And then there are the perks: you can use the swimming pools and the sports equipment and the theatre and cafés and things when you get time off, and (more interestingly) the *hidden* perks: you get to date the campers, with a bit of luck a different one every week as the visitors change! Just think, I could find myself having six and a bit holiday romances this summer.

James and I – well, things had got a bit weird between us before he went away. He didn't say anything about having to remain faithful for six months, so *I* didn't either, and his letters have got fewer and fewer over the weeks, so I don't really know what's going to happen there. Or how I actually feel about what might happen, come to that.

Mum just ran in here holding up a clutch of knickers.

'I can only find fourteen pairs!' she cried worriedly. 'Do you think someone ought to pop out and buy some more?'

'Mum, there's hot water where I'm going,' I said patiently. 'It's not the outer reachers of Upper Mongolia. And I expect they've even heard of washing powder.'

'I know, dear, but . . .'

'And if not, I can always go down to the stream and bang them on the rocks.'

'Now you're just being silly. I thought you might not have time to do all that.' She paused and brought something out

6

from behind her back. 'Now, about your vests . . .' she began hopefully.

I let out a horrified scream. 'Definitely, positively not! You'll make me the laughing stock of the camp.'

'Those sea breezes . . .' she murmured.

'Mum!'

'All right, dear,' she said, sighing heavily as she went out. She feels that she's failed as a mother unless she can get me into a vest occasionally.

Feel that I should have an early night, but I keep remembering things I haven't packed and jumping up again. Feel a bit nervous: I've never looked after a thousand people before; I hope they'll behave themselves

Saturday, 19th July

I'm sitting on my own little bed in my chalet. It's quite a small chalet, just two beds, a wardrobe and two chests of drawers, but there's a shower room and loo attached. Everything has robins on it – not the loo, I don't mean, but everything else: bedspreads, wallpaper, lampshades, with a big, grubby robin woven into the carpet.

When I look out of the window, all I can see are rows and rows of identical (staff) chalets and, right up at the end, the camp's first aid centre. To the left of that is the lost children's office and to the right, the nappy washing service. I hope the wind doesn't blow down from that direction very often!

The train journey here wasn't without its incidents. At the station this morning I poised myself gracefully on the train step for a quiet moment in which to gaze nostalgically at All I Was Leaving Behind, wearing my best dress and thinking that I looked *just* like someone boarding the Orient Express, when a huge fat man squeezed into a brown suit bowled up to me and roared: 'My first class carriage is an absolute tip!

You're a cleaner, aren't you? You ought to be hoist with your own wash leather!'

Gave him disdainful look. He obviously hadn't seen the Orient Express.

'Do you mind? I am *not* a cleaner,' I said in a frightfully posh voice, and I retired in a dignified way to my second class seat.

I decided that there were probably other new Robinson's staff on the train so I spent most of the journey going up and down the carriages playing Spot the Robin. Managed to tread on Fatty's toes twice. None of the spotted Robins *were* – in fact, I was the only Robinson's person there, so that was probably why there wasn't a courtesy bus to meet me at the other end. Walked from the station with half a ton of luggage and checked in at the personnel office, quietly gasping.

Mr Mettly, the staff officer, was very nice – showed me to my chalet and said my chalet-mate, another new Robin, would be here later. Today I've just got to walk round the camp and get the feel of everything, then there's a day's training tomorrow and we all (there are nine new-for-the-high-season Robins) start properly as fully-fledged (his joke) junior Robins on Monday.

It took me ages to walk round the camp and I got lost twice. There's everything here: an indoor pool and an outdoor pool, a children's fun pool, a games area, sports hall, amusement arcade, funfair, lots of shops, boating pool, ballroom where all the competitions are held, smaller ball-room that's a church on Sundays, theatre, betting shop and various restaurants, hamburger bars, cafés and pubs. It's just like a little town.

When I'd walked round a few times (watching the Robins closely to see how they were performing), I came back here to change out of the gear I'd travelled in. Decided to have a shower and was just coming out wrapped in a bath towel (with a robin on it) when someone crashed through the door yelling: 'Hi, I'm your chalet mate!'

. . . It was a *male* voice! I jumped back into the shower and peered round the corner.

'Hi!' I said in a nervous voice, clutching my bath towel for dear life.

The guy stared at me in astonishment. He was tall, eighteenish or so, and had black hair which stood up in front – looking at that moment as if it was standing up in shock.

'Well,' he said, 'I know they told us we'd have everything we wanted in the chalets, but this is a bit of a bonus.'

'I . . . er . . .' I said helpfully. Bonus indeed! I remembered I was wearing a vile pink-flowered shower hat (one of Mum's going-away presents) and whipped it off quickly.

'Perhaps there's some mistake,' he said. He looked down at the key in his hand. 'Is this chalet 35?'

I nodded, wondering what my hair looked like.

'Sorry!' he said, 'but you're obviously in the wrong place, aren't you?'

9

'*I* am? What about you?'

'Look, I've just come from the personnel office,' he said in the sort of voice which inferred he *knew* he was speaking to an idiot, 'they said chalet 35, gave me the key. It's obvious *you've* got it wrong.'

I bristled as best I could in a bath towel and stopped wondering what my hair looked like. 'No, *you've* got it wrong. This is my chalet. I've unpacked.'

'Then you'll have to re-pack, won't you?' he said. 'I don't want to be funny but I've had a long journey and I'm whacked out.'

I glowered at him. He was the best-looking guy I'd seen since I'd spotted that new assistant in the sports shop at home, but he was obviously a right pig. 'I AM STAYING HERE,' I said slowly and loudly.

'Then I hope that shower's big enough for two,' he said, 'because I'm coming in.'

I gave a squeak. 'Look, you're dressed,' I said hastily, 'you go down to the personnel office and tell them what's happened. There's got to be a mistake somewhere.'

He glowered back at me – his glower was nearly as good as mine, but not quite – and snatched up his case. 'Of course there's a mistake, and it's bound to be you who's made it!' he said. 'You females are all the same.'

'Well, just let me tell you . . .' I began, but he'd gone; picked up his case and slammed out.

I ran to the window and made faces at his back as he marched down between the chalets and back to the office. He almost had sparks coming out of his heels.

Fuming, I got dressed and sat on my bed waiting for him to come back and tell me what had happened and whether I had to change chalets. He hasn't come, though, and that's made me even madder. It's obviously him who's got it wrong and he hasn't got the decency to come back and apologise. Just *wait* until I see him again . . .

I walked round the camp once more and then I went up to the staff restaurant for something to eat. Didn't see him anywhere. The restaurant was packed and there was a generous scattering of real Robins in their red jumpers and brown skirts (not the men, I don't mean, they had trousers) and they all looked very jolly and friendly. They didn't take any notice of me in the corner – perhaps it's because they don't know I'm going to be a Robin. Once I get into my red woolly I'll be made. An instant member of the In crowd.

Came back to my chalet (where's my chalet-mate, then?), watched TV on the black and white portable provided and am now in bed. Feel a weeny bit homesick.

Oh yes, have just opened a packet Mum put in my case marked: 'For emergency use', hoping it was a nice slab of chocolate, and it was two new vests.

Sunday, 20th July

At ten o'clock this morning my chalet-mate arrived. She was wearing one of those wrap-around printed skirts, a t-shirt with a white dove on the front and a big gauze scarf thing wrapped right round her neck and flowing out behind her.

'Hi! Peace!' she said.

'And . . . er . . . peace to you, too,' I said, startled.

'I'm Rainbow.'

'Rainbow?' I croaked.

'Actually,' she said in a confidential whisper, 'my real name's Doreen because I was named after some old auntie, but if *you* were called Doreen, *you'd* change it, wouldn't you?'

I swallowed. 'I suppose I would.'

'What's your name?'

'Janey,' I said apologetically.

'Oh well.' She sat down on the nearest bed, bounced up and down a bit. 'You can't help that.'

'I was expecting you yesterday.'

11

She made a whistling noise through her teeth. 'Impossible,' she said. 'Very dodgy for me to travel. All the signs were wrong.'

'The road signs?' I asked, mystified.

'The astrological signs,' she said. 'Never travel when there are bad portents.'

'Right,' I said faintly. I was sharing with some sort of lunatic, that was obvious. 'You are . . . you are going to be a Robin?'

She nodded. 'I helped out at a camp near home last year – the same sort of job as this but I didn't live in.'

'Was it fun?'

'Great!' She stopped looking soulful and her eyes gleamed. 'Hard work but a real laugh.'

I relaxed a bit. Maybe she wasn't completely mad after all.

At half past ten we were summoned to a place called (I might have known) The Robins' Nest, to meet Mother Robin, a girl about twenty-five called Patty who was going to initiate us into the mysteries.

There are five new girl Robins: me, Rainbow, Michelle, Emma and Angela, and four boys: David, Leo, Jim and *him*, old pig, whose name has turned out to be Leslie.

He avoided looking at me all through the meeting, so I went straight up to him in the break and asked what had happened about the chalet.

'I was expecting to see you with an explanation,' I said frostily. 'I think you might have let me know what happened.'

'Oh, they'd spelled my name wrong on the form; they'd put me in the girls' chalets by mistake,' he said.

'So, you were wrong and I was right!'

'No, we were both right, *they* were wrong.'

'Well, whatever. You should at least have come back and told me.'

'Should have done, but I didn't,' he said, grinning. 'Aren't I the limit?'

12

'Yes, you *are*!' I snapped, 'I think you're probably the . . .'

'Robins!' Patty called in a voice all dripping with sweetness. 'Remember that a Robin is charming at all times.'

'Someone not too far away will find that extremely difficult,' I muttered under my breath.

Anyway, what the meeting revealed was that our only real duty as Robins is to keep the campers happy. We have to mingle with them at all times, chat to them, join in their games, play with their children, give them directions to wherever they want to go and generally be little rays of sunshine in their lives. We've also got to be prepared to help out anywhere in emergencies – like if they get short-staffed in the nursery or the shops. We'll be on duty all day and all evening with one day off a week.

'But you'll be enjoying yourself so it won't be tiring,' Patty finished. She smiled at us kindly. 'Now, what you've got to remember is that a Robin is a perky, friendly little bird and you should be like Robins all the time. A Robin will give a friendly little chirrup to everyone he meets!'

I made a snorting noise and Patty looked at me beadily. I think I was supposed to have taken her seriously.

In the afternoon we acted little scenes with other Robins playing 'difficult campers' to show how we could cope with them, and at four o'clock we went to collect our red jumpers and skirts; three of each.

'There's one last thing,' Patty said, supervising the Giving of the Jumper ceremony. 'Every week one of you will be awarded the golden feather – for the Robin who makes the biggest contribution to a camper's happiness!' She paused and beamed round at us, 'I just know that you'll *all* want to win that golden feather every week!'

I managed to push down another snort. 'What about the other end of the scale?' I whispered to Rainbow, '. . . the stale crust award? For the Robin who's laziest or . . .'

'Or who pecks a camper,' Rainbow said quietly beside me.

'Certainly not,' Patty said severely. 'No Robin is *ever* lazy.'

Later we all went up to the canteen together where Rainbow and I swopped life stories and I decided she wasn't mad at all, just a bit dippy. As well as the astrology bit, she's a vegetarian and won't eat meat or anything even remotely connected with an animal, like eggs or milk. Seems the staff canteen have got a bit of a challenge on their hands.

Stayed frostily apart from Les, though did hear him say to David in the queue that he thought it was daft they should call the guys Robins, that it was a bit wet.

'I suppose *you* think you ought to be called something macho – an Eagle or a Vulture?' I said sarcastically.

'Good idea,' he said. 'I think I'll put it to them. I'm much more a Golden Eagle than a Robin.'

I made an explosive noise and turned disdainfully away. Conceited twit!

Came back to the chalet to write to Mum and Dad and generously included Richard. Wonder how they're all managing without me and how Jimmy is.

14

I'll write to James tomorrow. Or the next day.

Quite fancied an early night but Rainbow had to do an awful lot of things before we could go to sleep. First of all she wanted her bed turned so that she'd wake up facing East. We tried to do this but after heaving and struggling and fighting to get it round we discovered that the legs of the bed were screwed to the floor (obviously they've had naughty Robins with sticky fingers here in the past. Wonder how they got their stolen beds home on the train?)

After that we had the creaming on of the face emulsions.

'All the products I use are natural ones and none have been tested on animals,' Rainbow said loftily, patting her face all over with goo.

I peered into the jar at something brown, lumpy and disgusting-looking.

'I'm not surprised,' I said, 'no self-respecting rabbit would be seen with *that* on its face.'

'You use synthetic rubbish, full of additives and perfume,

do you?' she asked, looking at me pityingly. 'I should say goodbye to your skin right now, if I were you.'

Before I could say anything, she was announcing loftily, 'I need to do some yoga and commune with my inner self.'

She went into a headstand but, as I pointed out, she had one leg resting on the wall and the other kept touching the door so she wasn't *really* supporting herself. Helped her as much as possible by shouting:

'You're going wobbly! You're slipping! Mind you don't collapse on to my synthetic beauty products!' so she didn't stay upside down for long.

The evening finished with her chanting what she called a Mantra; apparently this is a word that means a lot to you, repeated over and over again until you fall asleep or until your room-mate throws something at you.

Her word was *Vegetable*. It might sound an OK, harmless sort of word but when you've heard it two thousand or so times it can get on your nerves a tiny bit. Decided to start up a Mantra of my own in opposition and picked the word *Chocolate*. She packed up saying *Vegetable* on about my hundred and forty-ninth *Chocolate*.

Monday, 21st July

First day as a Robin. Rainbow and I set off at the same time for breakfast (she looking quite ordinary and human in her red woolly) and met Michelle and Emma on the way there. Michelle is small and fluffy and had a historical romance under her arm (don't know when she'll find time to read *that*) and Emma is tall, earnest, and looks as if she'll make sure people have a good holiday whether they want one or not.

Rainbow caused a stir in the canteen; she couldn't eat eggs, bacon, sausages or even cereal because it had to have milk on it. In the end she settled for a small piece of brown toast, no butter.

'I don't know how you can bear to eat animal flesh,' she said, looking disdainfully at my plate. A moment after that she sniffed the air; 'What's that gorgeous smell?'

'Fried bacon,' I said, 'all lovely and crispy. Want to try a piece of mine?'

'Certainly not,' she said, but I noticed her giving my plate sidelong glances and sniffing in a longing sort of way all through breakfast.

After we'd finished eating we all set off in different directions; me towards the fairground where I spent all morning going up and down on the merry-go-round horses, taking toddlers on the helter skelter and feeling sick on the octopus. Don't mind if I don't see another fairground ride for ten years or so. By the end of the morning my new red jumper had got dirt, candy floss, ice cream and a large piece of chewing gum stuck to the front . . . but did Auntie Robin complain or lose her cheery smile? No, she did not.

Twice Les went by, both times with some young lady camper in tow. He smiled at me smugly both times: overbearing, conceited idiot.

In the afternoon I patrolled the children's theatre and watched 'Music and Fun with Auntie Bertie and her Magic Rabbit'. Two children were sick and had to be taken back to their chalets. Another jumper gone.

Tuesday, 22nd July

I have fallen in love. I think. He is a lifeguard at the children's fun pool and was standing very manfully by the edge blowing on a whistle and trying to stop two children drowning each other when I saw him. Stopped and stared and then noticed that Michelle was already there, also staring in a stupified way.

'He's just like a young Richard Gere,' she said breathlessly when I went over to her. 'Look at that face . . . those muscles . . . that blond hair.'

17

'What's his name?' I asked in a hushed whisper, as if we were in the presence of a minor god.

'Mike,' she said. 'Mike and Michelle . . . they sound kind-of right together, don't they?'

'D'you think so?' I asked politely.

I think it was then she noticed I was smitten, too, because she suddenly looked me up and down as if summing me up.

'Have you got a boyfriend at home?' she asked.

'Sort of,' I said. 'At least, I would have but he's in Germany. Anyway, it was getting a bit funny . . .' My voice trailed away, I didn't know how to explain what had happened between me and James. It had been all wonderful at first, then not quite so wonderful, then not wonderful at all – and I still didn't know whether to hang about and see if it was going to get good again or what.

'Oh, if I had someone at home I'd *never* be unfaithful,' she said in a goody-goody voice, and before I could reply, dashed off to mop up a dad who'd got soaked by a little dear on the Squirty Splash machine.

Went up boldly to ask lifeguard what the time was.

'Er . . . it may have escaped your notice but I'm only wearing swimming trunks,' he said, smiling at me in a wonderful way.

Went red. 'So you are,' I said.

'Are you new?'

I nodded. 'I started yesterday.'

'Like it?'

'So far,' I said.

'Well, I expect I'll see you around the old place,' he said. 'What's your name, by the way?'

I told him and a second or two later he dashed away to pull out a red-haired boy trying to swim with armbands on his feet.

Playing the dutiful Robin, I swooped on a pile of discarded paper cups and sweet wrappers and carried them off in the

18

direction of Porky the Paper Eater ('Children – let Porky make a Pig of himself!') passing Michelle on the way.

She looked at me suspiciously. 'Been talking about anything interesting?' she asked in her soft little voice.

'This and that. He said he'd see me around soon,' I added carelessly, and had the pleasure of seeing her turn pale green as I walked away.

In the afternoon I had to help out at the Bonny Baby Contest in the ballroom. It was murderous; Patty had already told me that each of the mums would be quite convinced that her baby was the bonniest (and that means fattest) of the lot and there wouldn't be anything anyone could do to convince her otherwise.

The judges were the local vicar, one of the stars from the Robinson's Nite-Nite Show and a nurse, and my job was to escort each mum and baby from the front row to the stage, where the judges were waiting to coo at the babies and size them up. Back in the audience were the baby's dad and any aunties, uncles or grandmas that had come on holiday with it, and they all sat there and muttered rebelliously if the judges seemed to spend more time cooing at anyone other than *their* baby.

Today there were fourteen babies in various stages of fatness including one huge red-faced bald one that I could hardly lift up. As I put each one down on the lambskin in front of the judges, it would start crying and then the others would let out a fresh bawl in sympathy, so at the end there was a whole gang of babies screaming their heads off.

I had to take the marks from the judges and hand them to Patty, in charge, then she read the winners out in reverse order, just like a beauty competition.

Of course, the only people who agreed with the results were the ones whose baby had won; the other mums snatched up their still yelling offspring and marched out in a huff. The mother of the huge bald one came up to me just as I was

19

making a discreet exit (and planning to be unavailable next Tuesday afternoon).

'Look at him! Just look at him, will you?' she said, thrusting him at me. 'What's wrong with him, that's what I want to know.'

I looked at him. I didn't know where to start.

'Nothing at all,' I lied, patting his bald head and hoping his nose wasn't going to run on me. 'He's a real little darling.'

'He is, isn't he?' said his mum aggressively. 'Why didn't he win, then?'

I held him gingerly; he was wearing one of those plastic bibs and there was a lot of dribble in the bottom of it. 'I really couldn't say,' I said, 'some people obviously don't know a . . . er . . . lovely baby when they see one.'

'I mean, that winner was like a skinned rabbit! He wasn't a lovely porker like my Jeremy.'

'Quite,' I said, and I patted the screaming Jeremy again and handed him back.

'I think he likes his Auntie Robin,' his mum said fondly.

A few moments later I found a big damp patch along my arm where he'd been sitting. That's another red jumper done for.

Wednesday, 23rd July

Am getting into the swing of things; feel as if I've been a Robin for ages now. The time passes really quickly because there's so much going on and you're always busy; even when you're supposed to be having free time and you creep off to try and write a letter home or read a book or something, one of the campers will find you and you'll hear: 'Excuse me, you are a Robin, aren't you? I wondered if . . .'

I wrote to James this morning, giving him my address here so he could write back. It was hard, writing to him; it's difficult to know what to say to someone who you've once been really close to and now aren't. Everytime I tried to picture him I couldn't remember his face, I just kept seeing someone with blond streaks and a pair of red swimming trunks. I thought I'd love James for ever and ever, too. Funny, that.

There's not much in the way of fanciable holiday-makers in the camp this week. Marcy, one of the 'long-term' Robins, says it's a No. 5 week – dead as far as boys are concerned. Some weeks, No. 1 weeks, you get loads in, apparently, and other weeks it's mostly families and fat babies.

Rainbow's just burst into the chalet to tell me she's got a date with someone called Kevin, who's the assistant catering manager. Apparently she got to know him by making such a fuss in the canteen about what she can and can't eat. *Now* they've got in a whole lot of new things just for her: muesli and carrot jam and lentils, yukky stuff like that.

'I'm teaching him all about wholefoods,' she said.

'Who wants food with holes in it?' I asked, bemused.

'Wholefoods with a "W". Everyone should eat more of them,' she said, nibbling at something that looked like a lump of old wood. She said it was a carob bar – 'full of delicious vitamins'.

I'd brought in a very large cream slice with icing covering the top and she made a face at it and said that if I carried on eating rubbish, my body would be sure to rebel.

Ate it all up greedily, then looked down at my body and wondered which bit was going to go first. It all looked quite quiet, so I licked my lips and fingers and went for a shower. When I came back in I made for the cardboard box the slice had been in, meaning to eat the huge blob of cream that had escaped on to the lid – but the blob had mysteriously disappeared.

Looked at Rainbow suspiciously. 'Have you eaten a big lump of cream?' I asked her.

She blinked at me. 'Would I be likely to do *that*?' she said in a shocked voice. 'You know I never touch animal products.'

'I know,' I said. Maybe it just kind of evaporated into thin air.

Thursday, 24th July

Spent nearly all day at the First Aid post. I was coming out of the small ballroom after trying to encourage a few people to join in the Old Tyme Dancing and failing miserably, when a boy came up to me and asked if I knew where he could find a doctor.

'For you?' I said. I'd seen the boy around a bit; he was about fifteen, I suppose, and on holiday with his mum and dad and dead embarrassed about it.

He nodded and I noticed he was holding his arm in a funny way and there was a trickle of blood coming from his forehead. 'What have you done?' I asked, leading him towards the medical centre.

'I was trying to escape and go into town,' he said. 'I jumped off the top of the wall and fell all wrong.'

I didn't like to laugh. 'You don't have to escape!' I said. 'You can go out of the front gate.'

'Yeah, well, I didn't know that,' he said miserably.

He said his arm was painful and so was his ankle; he was limping a bit so we couldn't walk quickly. We were just passing the amusement arcade when old pig features Les came out, took one look at us and grinned. 'I know times are bad for you girls, but it's come to something when you've got to knock a fella about to get him to go out with you!' he said.

I silenced him with *A Look*. What a creep!

When we got to the First Aid post it was decided that the boy should go off to hospital to be X-rayed, so one of the nurses took him (she was a pretty eighteen-year-old; suddenly he looked quite cheered-up), and because they were short-staffed, I volunteered to take her place on the desk.

Spent the day looking at cut knees, blisters, twisted ankles and insect bites and ushering their owners into the nurses.

23

Sister-in-charge told me they'd delivered a baby there the week before. Glad I missed that.

On the way back this evening I spent an hour on the boating lake taking children for a row. It's quite a big lake with an island in the middle containing a plastic log cabin and a dozen or so assorted wild animals: hippos and alligators and shiny brown dinosaur-looking things. Rowed round to the other side, where the children's fun pool is, and saw Mike with Michelle hovering around him. Every time I've seen Mike lately she's been in the background somewhere, batting her eyelashes and looking fluffy. How am I going to get anywhere with *her* always around?

Got a letter from Mum telling me everything that was going on at home and enclosing a muddy paw-print from Jimmy. (Sometimes I think she's as silly as I am.) She said to make sure my woolly jumpers weren't washed in biological powder or 'it'll bring you up in a nasty rash', to make sure all my underwear was rinsed four times 'if not you may find yourself with a problem You Know Where'. She also said I must remember to eat plenty of fresh greens or I'd get spots round the mouth and drink milk or my fingernails would all break off. In capitals at the bottom it said: HEAVILY SPICED FOOD MAY GIVE VIOLENT INDIGESTION.

I think that unless I go home with at least leprosy she's going to be severely disappointed.

Tonight Rainbow and I went to the club on site (called *The Nesting Box*) so she could show Kevin off to me. I was expecting some raving hippie – at any rate, someone with long hair tied back in a tail and wearing a t-shirt with *Save the Bats* on it, but to my surprise he was quite ordinary: tallish, with short brown hair and dark eyes with a hint of the Sylvester Stallones about them.

He told me it was his third season at Robinson's but his first time at this camp; he'd started off just as a kitchen assistant straight from college and worked his way up.

'Most of us permanent staff have worked at other camps before,' he said.

'I suppose you don't know a lifeguard called Michael?' I asked hopefully.

He nodded. 'Sure. Mike and I started here on the same day.'

'Oooh!' I said.

Rainbow sipped at her carrot juice thoughtfully. 'Could you arrange a foursome, d'you think?' she said after a moment. 'Always provided you've found out Mike's birthday so I can see if he and Janey are compatible.'

'Never mind that!' I said. 'I'll take him whatever he is.'

Friday, 25th July

Actually saw Mike this morning when I was going into breakfast, but he didn't see me. Funny how little I *do* see of him, actually, probably because the staff canteen is enormous and *everyone* goes there. The whole Robinson's 'behind-the-scenes' staff: office workers, cleaners, maintenance men, catering staff, shop assistants, entertainment and bar staff, chalet maids – as well as all the Robins, of course.

Had to help out in one of the shops today because, being

the end of the week, it was Shopping for Souvenirs day. Campers could choose between brass ornaments with robins on, wooden spoons with robins on, ashtrays with robins on, tea-towels with robins on or plastic snowstorms with robins *in*. Did a roaring trade in wooden spoons, sold thousands. Discovered later that I'd sold them for fifteen pence each when it should have been forty-five.

In the afternoon I was in the ballroom for the last competition of the week, the Fat 'n' Fun competition. All you've got to do to enter is be big, and laugh a lot. Didn't think anyone would want to go in for something like that but found out it was one of the most popular competitions of the week; the stage was positively groaning under the weight of large women walking up and down being hearty and hilarious.

It was won by the largest one of all – a vast woman in a green lurex dress who clasped one of the judges (the vicar, again) to her bosom and nearly suffocated him. She won a small silver cup with a (fat) robin on it.

After that was the general prizegiving for all the competitions that had been held that week, including the children's swimming races and gymnastics and all sorts of competitions I'd never known were on, like the Men's Knobbly Knees, the Party Girl of the Week, the Pop Star Look-Alike (got quite excited about that one but it was won by someone who looked like Max Bygraves) and the Dads and Lads, whatever *that* is. Patty told me that some of the campers come to Robinson's just to go in for the competitions; they don't sit around or swim or tan themselves, just come to the ballroom and go in for whatever they can.

My job was to retrieve the prizewinners from the audience and walk him or her up to the stage to receive their cup or whatever from the entertainments manager, Mr Waller. Everyone's photograph was taken ready to be sent home to their local paper where they would be celebrities for a day or two. Perhaps *that's* the attraction in winning.

26

Saw Leslie in the audience sitting first with Miss Lovely Legs and then with Miss Personality. He never misses a trick, that one.

Went back to the chalet to find Rainbow tucking into a food parcel from home.

'I wrote and told Mum and Dad you were all cannibals here and they sent me some *real* food,' she explained. 'Want a sesame seed bar?'

I looked at it. 'No thanks,' I said, getting a bar of fruit and nut out of my bedside cabinet and setting about it.

'Mmm. Delicious,' she said, munching some awful-looking green stuff. 'Dried seaweed is *so* good for you.' She looked at me severely, 'You're pale, you know. What you need is some wheatgerm.'

I made a face. 'It sounds horrible,' I said, 'as if it's got six legs and crawls up you when you're not looking.'

'You sprinkle it on your food,' she said earnestly. 'It's really marvellous.' She eyed the chocolate, fast disappearing. 'Chocolate poisons the system, you know that?'

I popped another two pieces into my mouth. 'But what a delicious way to go.'

Went to have the last couple of pieces when I'd had a shower but they'd gone. Suppose I must have eaten them without knowing it.

Saturday, 26th July

Changeover day for the campers with about 900 of them moving out and another 900 moving in. Nearly everyone stays just a week, apparently, but a lot of them have another week later in the year, or at Christmas.

They're supposed to be out by ten o'clock to enable the chalets to be cleaned and spruced-up ready for the next lot of arrivals at three o'clock, and in the middle of all the packing they usually discover they've lost half the stuff they came with; I kept getting despatched down to Old Jay in the lost property office for a swimsuit or a pair of shorts or a t-shirt, usually described very vaguely as 'a bluey colour, size 12ish. Or it might have been size 14'. Once we had three women fighting over the same plain black *new*-looking bikini, while two other limp and faded black bikinis sat unwanted on the side. They all swore the new one was theirs.

Apart from the army of cleaning ladies, the camp was strangely empty after eleven o'clock, so Michelle, Rainbow, Emma and I had a very long and lazy lunch hour. Michelle was mostly engrossed in a historical novel with a picture of a medieval king looking uncannily like Michael J. Fox on the front.

'Those were the days,' she said, finishing it at last. She looked at the rest of us all misty-eyed, 'guys were so romantic, then.'

'What, always rescuing maidens from castles and all that?' Rainbow asked.

She nodded dreamily – and just then Kevin appeared from the depths of the kitchens.

'It's all on for tomorrow,' he said to me and Rainbow. 'I've seen Mike and got it fixed up.'

'Great,' I said, not daring to look at Michelle.

'What's that, then?' she asked when he'd gone back to his thousand hot dinners.

'A . . . er . . . foursome,' I said.

'With Mike?'

I nodded. 'Kevin knows him, you see. They're close friends and he arranged it.'

'Oh,' she said forlornly, and I felt quite sorry for her.

'Maybe he won't like me,' I said, crossing my fingers behind my back.

Felt a bit guilty about James right then, too, but reminded myself that he hadn't exactly been showering me with letters declaring his undying love since he went to Germany.

After lunch I was walking back to do a spot of washing when I heard a baby crying in one of the chalets that the cleaners were working towards. I went in and there was a baby sitting in its cot and banging on the bars, yelling nearly as loudly as one of the Bonny Baby contestants. Well, I knew it couldn't belong to one of the new lot of campers, they weren't in yet, so that meant it must have been left behind by one of the lot that had gone that morning. An abandoned baby!

I picked it up and it stopped crying; I took it to Reception to report it and then went on to the nursery. We were just pulling the parents to pieces: 'Who would abandon a dear little baby like this?' 'What a *wicked* thing to do!' 'How *could* they?' when a woman ran in, crying in a distracted sort of way.

'My Hannah!' she said, grabbing the baby off one of the nurses.

'She couldn't go through with it!' the chief nursery nurse whispered to me. 'She couldn't live with the guilt!'

The woman burst into tears. 'My husband thought I'd put her in the carry cot in the car, and I thought *he* had. We were halfway home before we realised that neither of us had!'

When I got back to my chalet, Reception had delivered a letter from James – Mum had sent it on from home. I put it on the side and fiddled about a bit to waste time, not wanting to open it. Well, if he said he missed me like mad, couldn't live another moment without me and was coming down to claim me – and in the meantime I wasn't to look at anyone else, I'd be cooked. If he said that, then I wouldn't, *couldn't* go out with Mike. Well, I could but it would all be spoilt because I'd feel so guilty about it.

After about ten minutes I couldn't find anything else to fiddle with, so I had to open it.

It was a 'Dear Janey'. He said he thought our relationship had pretty much run its course, and though he wanted to stay 'really good friends' with me, he reckoned we both ought to be free to go out with other people.

Felt incensed and pleased and miserable and furious all at once. Well, it was exactly what I'd been thinking, but I'd wanted to be the one to say it. Now he's gone and done it first I can't help feeling slightly panic-stricken. Maybe I do love him after all . . .

Took a walk round the field clutching his letter and trying to feel lost and abandoned and tragic. Practised a few long-drawn-out sighs but they were a bit half-hearted. Feel I should be able to get *some* drama out of the situation, though. Why is it I don't feel anything much?

After I got fed up with being lost and soulful I went over to Reception where it seemed 900 people had descended all at the same time. Did my best to be helpful and charming for four hours and then went back to the chalet, exhausted.

Roll on tomorrow. My first day off *and* a date with Mike.

Sunday, 27th July

Am writing this sitting up in bed with Rainbow giggling beside me. Can't believe she knew nothing about it – in fact I've told her I'm going to call her Doreen all week to try and get my own back.

To start from the beginning: we had a nice, quiet day washing things and writing home and reading the papers and keeping out of all the new campers' way. At sevenish we showered and changed ready to meet Kevin and Mike in town and go ice-skating.

Felt really excited and nervous. Couldn't remember when I'd been looking forward to something so much: when I first went out with James, I suppose.

'Hope the stars are all right for tonight,' I said to Rainbow as we waited on the steps of the ice rink.

'I'm not sure,' she said cautiously. 'I'll have to do a proper chart for you; see if you and Mike are compatible.'

'I'm only going skating with him,' I said, 'not up the aisle.'

'Funny, though ... there was something not quite right when I looked in my big astrology book.'

'Never mind all that rubbish – isn't that them getting off the bus?' I said. Well, I could see it was Kevin all right, but Mike looked sort of different.

They came nearer; I began to panic. 'I don't think that's him!' I said. 'It's not Mike!'

'Of course it's Mike,' she said. 'They're good friends, aren't they? Kevin wouldn't have brought anyone else.'

'He's got bigger and fatter, then! He's dyed his hair black and it's all greasy!' I said, my voice rising in horror. 'He's wearing a purple nylon t-shirt! It's not the right one!'

'Oh, yipes!' she said, and then they were up to us and it was too late for me to make a run for it.

'Hi, girls!' Kevin said. 'This is Mike. Mike, meet Janey, someone who's been *dying* to meet you!'

I gulped. Mike put out a hand and slapped me on the back. 'Hello, darlin',' he said, 'always pleased to meet an admirer!'

I looked at him and lost all power of speech. As well as the purple nylon t-shirt he had black denim jeans, a heavy studded belt and a tattoo saying 'Kim 4 Ever' halfway up his arm.

'Well, isn't this great?' Kevin said, probably thinking I was silent because I was overcome with passion. 'Here we are out of camp and all set for a great night!'

I shot Rainbow a look, a sort of 'rescue me' look. She shot back a 'well, what can *I* do?' look.

It was probably the worst date I've ever had. Mike II was awful; big and loud and fell all over the ice tripping up as many people as he could when he did so. His hair dropped into greasy strands over his eyes when he fell and he'd then spend ten minutes by the side of the rink, combing it back in front of one of the mirrors.

'It's the wrong one!' I hissed to Kevin when Mike disappeared for the first comb. 'He's not the one from the children's pool!'

'Children's pool? He works at the indoor pool,' Kevin said. 'I thought that's where you'd seen him.'

'If I'd seen him there I would have run in the other direction,' I said. 'He's awful!'

Kevin spread his hands, looking bewildered. 'Well, how was I supposed to know?' he said.

A sickly smile spread across my face as Mike came back to us, hair flicked into place. 'Having a good time, darlin'?' he asked. 'It's all right here, innit?'

I nodded. I didn't trust myself to speak.

Got through the evening somehow and managed to avoid any suggestion of a goodnight kiss by starting a sudden bout of hayfever just as our chalet came into view. Had to rush in to take my medicine, shouting 'Thanks for a lovely evening!' over my shoulder.

'I'll kill you for this,' I said to Rainbow when she came in. 'I'll force-feed you with a fillet steak.'

'It's not my fault,' she said. 'I told you the stars didn't look right.'

Monday, 28th July

Spent a good part of today avoiding Mike II. From never seeing him before, suddenly he keeps popping up everywhere I go, winking at me, shouting 'Wotcha, darlin'!' or just leering quietly across the ballroom.

Even Les has noticed, said something about 'your admirer with the tattoo' at lunchtime in the canteen. Gave him another Look.

Went to the kitchens this afternoon to find Kevin.

'You'll have to tell Mike I don't fancy him, that it was all a mistake!' I said, catching him behind half a ton of peeled, glistening chips.

'I'll try,' he said, 'but he's rather got it into his head that you're eating your heart out for him.'

'Oh, God!' I wailed. I hesitated, 'Couldn't you get to know the other one?' I said wheedlingly. 'The right one?'

'No fear,' he said. 'I've done all the match-making I'm ever going to do! Now, if you'll excuse me . . .'

I looked round and shuddered; about five hundred fish had just come up on a vast trolley affair and were lying there watching me with dead glassy eyes.

Spent most of the afternoon helping with a children's treasure hunt (Auntie Bertie's Magic Rabbit had disappeared, the naughty thing) and then placating a woman who said she didn't like her chalet, she wanted something better.

'In the brochure they had pink curtains,' she said. 'Pink curtains and a fur rug next to the bed.'

'I'll see what I can do,' I promised. Went off to see the accommodation manager and he hunted everywhere and finally found her a fur rug. The woman was only slightly appeased. 'Such a pity about the curtains,' she niggled as I left.

Walked back past the children's pool (funny how my feet just happen to go that way) where real Mike was just coming off duty. He spoke! He asked me how I was getting on and if I'd enjoyed ice-skating last night; he'd seen me going in with Kevin, Rainbow and Mike II! I tried desperately to think of a way of letting him know that I wasn't actually *with* Mike II, that it had all been a dreadful mistake, but couldn't think of how to put it. Now he probably thinks I go for the purple nylon t-shirt type.

Worse was to come – at dinner time Michelle said she'd seen us going past her chalet at eleven o'clock.

'Do you know, when you said you were going with Mike, I

thought you meant the lifeguard on the children's pool,' she said, all smiles and breathless little sighs. '*Such* a relief when I saw who it really was.' She hesitated. 'Tell me, do you really like that type?' she asked after a moment. 'Each to her own, I suppose.'

It's not my day. Later on I tried to write to James but after six attempts, gave up. Couldn't decide whether to be:

1. Old Hollywood movieish: 'It was beautiful while it lasted. Thanks for the memory; I'll never forget you . . .'
2. Painfully hurt but determined to put on brave face: 'Oh well, if you think that's for the best then that's what we'd better do . . .'
3. Frightfully jolly and relieved: 'Do you know, it's *such* a coincidence, I was just about to write the same thing to you . . .'

Tuesday, 29th July

Little pep talk this morning from Patty.

'It's come to my attention that not all my Robins keep their smiles on!' she said. 'We've had a couple of complaints from campers that one Robin actually walked past them without saying hello!'

Shocked silence as we all took in this startling piece of news. I've discovered that not being cheeky and chirpy is the worst sin a Robin can commit. I watched Patty once going across the ballroom and she chirruped to the left and right at everyone she passed, looking for all the world like a demented budgie. That's how we're all supposed to be all the time. It doesn't matter if you feel ill, have been jilted the day before your wedding or your granny's been run over: none of that must show.

'Our campers look forward to coming here all year,' Patty said. 'For some of them it's the only break in routine they have; we provide the few days of happiness in their dull lives.'

'Cue to play violins . . .' Rainbow muttered beside me.

'I know that some of you have already decided that you can't stand the pace,' Patty went on. 'This is quite understandable and we always take on extra Robins at the beginning to cover those who'll leave.'

'Who's gone?' I asked, looking round.

'Angela and David,' Patty said. 'They decided that being a Robin wasn't for them.'

'You next?' Les said to me.

I smiled at him sweetly. 'I'm nominating you, actually.'

Spent most of the rest of the day first in the children's theatre, then the adult one.

In the children's I watched Auntie Bertie and the silly old Magic Rabbit again (he didn't seem nearly so magical this time round). When Auntie Bertie pretended she was going to eat him for tea a child burst into tears and nothing could stop her crying, so I had to take her out and walk her round the camp looking for her mum and dad. They were relaxing by the pool and weren't a *bit* pleased to see her; they looked at me as if they thought I'd brought her back deliberately to spoil their fun.

In the evening I saw 'It's Cabaret Time at Robinson's!' with jugglers and musicians and comedians. I had to show people to their seats and then show them out again when they'd had enough. Campers don't stay anywhere long because there's quite a lot going on in the evenings and as they're usually only here a week it's an effort to get everything in. There's a film, the big competitions with dancing afterwards, variety shows, bingo and a disco and floor show every night, so campers are usually to be seen rushing distractedly from one thing to the next, frightened of not getting their money's worth.

Saw Mike II on my way back to the chalet; he was coming along singing 'Viva España' very loudly – found out later from Rainbow that he'd done a turn at 'Your Robins' Own

Talent Nite'. Quickly ducked behind an ice cream kiosk so that he wouldn't see me.

Can't stop thinking of real Mike. Everytime I've seen him he's looked more hunky and wonderful. Perhaps if I got into difficulties in the ten centimetres of water in the children's pool he'd have to dive in and rescue me.

Wednesday, 30th July

Woke up early this morning; the natives were restless. When I looked out of the chalet window I saw a family of seven (gran, mum and dad and four children) all going off towards the camp centre. Sleepily wondered why, but later, on my way to breakfast, noticed that there were seven towels laid out on the front deckchairs by the outdoor pool to secure the best positions.

I clambered back into bed quietly so as not to wake Rainbow, who was snoring gently, and lay there for a while thinking of my room at home and stirring up a bit of homesickness. Our chalet's really tatty (mind you, it's looking a lot tattier since we arrived) and there's just no room for anything. I thought I was untidy but Rainbow's worse – the whole place is buried under tights, bits of make-up, half-empty shampoo bottles, books on astrology, leaflets on factory farming and small pieces of coloured hair ribbon – with a generous scattering of sunflower seeds over the top.

It's cramped, too: when you get out of bed you either knock your head on the wall in front of you or turn round and crack your shin on the bedstead.

Sighed and thought longingly of my room at home with the sheepskin rug Jimmy sleeps on if I can smuggle him up the stairs, my new pink and white duvet cover, my file of reminders of boys I've been out with (always good for shedding a few tears over) and my Bunnikins Burrow bedside light which Mum bought for me when I was thirteen. I didn't have the heart to tell her I was too old for things like that – and anyway, I quite like it.

After I'd finished wallowing and feeling nostalgic I wrote in my head the letter to James and then fished about under the bed for some notepaper and wrote the real thing.

I made it the type 3 – frightfully jolly. Well, I wouldn't want him to go round thinking he'd broken my heart, or, even worse, telling other people he had.

It was quite a hectic day when I eventually got up – ending tonight with me helping out first at the Ladies Darts Tournament and then the Lowest Limbo Competition, which must come pretty high on the list for being the most gruesomely embarrassing thing I've ever seen.

I thought it would only be young, very fit types going in for it but the entrants were anything but that: doddering old grandads, dads who pretended to be funny and *jumped* over the pole at the last minute – anyone determined to make a fool of themselves, in other words.

I watched one woman leave her two teenage daughters sitting in the audience and go up. Her dress wasn't really made for limbo dancing: it was short, tight and plunge-front. Her two daughters – I couldn't decide if they were pillar-box red or maybe just a shade darker – slouched down very low in their chairs and refused to speak to their mum when she came back.

Thursday, 31st July

Patty came bustling up after breakfast and asked if a Robin would go and chat to the campers and encourage them to go into the gymnasium for Keep Fit – apparently the instructor in charge was getting discouraged because not enough campers were turning up.

'Just go and talk nicely to them as they come out of the breakfast hall,' she beamed, her smile stretching almost to breaking point. 'Remind them that a few gentle exercises will make them feel good and help them to enjoy their holiday more.'

I volunteered, pinned a replica of Patty's smile on my face and went down to nab someone.

'Morning!' I said cheerfully to a stout middle-aged man.

'How about a few exercises to tone you up and get you feeling good?'

'I *am* feeling good,' he said, pulling in his paunch. 'And there's no part of me as needs toning, as you put it.'

'No, of course not,' I said hastily, moving away.

'Would you er . . . care to do a few gentle exercises?' I asked a younger man and his wife.

'No we would not!' she said. 'We're supposed to be here on holiday.'

Six couples later I was getting dispirited – they all seemed to take my asking them if they'd like to go and exercise as a personal insult.

Emma came up just as I was wondering whether anyone would know if I slunk away.

'You need to be more positive!' she said heartily. 'Make them think they've *got* to go, that it's all part of the holiday.'

'But I don't like . . .'

But she was already off and grabbing a granny.

'Just think – you'll be able to go home from your holiday feeling twenty years younger!' she enthused.

The little grey-haired lady looked up at her apprehensively.

'A few rousing exercises will put you on top of the world! Let's just go along to the gym, shall we?'

'But I . . .'

'Bring your husband if you like – the more the merrier!'

'But he's dead,' the little old lady said.

Emma looked taken-aback, but only for a moment. 'Then come on your own!' she said brightly. 'Who knows, perhaps we can fix you up with someone new.'

I watched, amazed and awe-struck, as Emma frog-marched her down the road and towards the gym. Two minutes later she was back again and rounding up a family group of six to march up there.

I melted away . . . she was doing a far better job than I could ever do. To be a Robin you should be a cross between a TV game show compère, a sergeant-major and a graduate from a charm school. Sometimes I feel a bit inadequate.

This afternoon I went back to the chalet to find Rainbow and Kevin sitting on the step outside and having a heated argument about astrology.

'You *would* say that, you've got your moon in Taurus!' she was saying as I stepped over them.

Later on I asked her if she was serious about him.

'I might be,' she said, 'if I could get him to change his disgusting habits.'

My ears pricked up. Did he bite his toenails? Comb his hair over food? Wipe his nose on his sleeve? 'What's he do, then?' I asked.

'He eats meat,' she said in a disgusted voice.

Told her I'd written to James and that I was now, officially, a Free Agent, so if anyone (e.g. Mike I) asked about me, I was available.

I only ever seem to see glimpses of him – it's never long enough to get anything going. Life's so rushed here and the days pass so quickly; if I'm not careful it'll be time to go home and I won't have had a holiday romance.

Friday, 1st August

At lunchtime most of the campers were fully occupied with what they like doing best – eating – so I decided to go back to my chalet and rinse out a few bits and pieces. Was just going past the amusement arcade when I heard a hugely loud and appreciative sort of wolf-whistle.

Glanced modestly round – I couldn't look insulted and women's libbish as I would have done at home in case it was a camper – but I couldn't see anyone. It came again, even louder. Maybe we'd had a new intake of campers – one of them was this incredible guy who'd fallen madly in love with

41

me at first glance and didn't know how to express himself any other way . . .

I turned again, ready to be swept off my feet . . . and saw Les coming out of the arcade laughing so hard he could hardly stand up.

'What's so funny?' I asked coldly. Surely it hadn't been *him* whistling?

'Only you!' he managed to croak out between guffaws. 'Only you and your admirer!'

'I suppose it was you being coarse and whistling in that vulgar way, was it?' I said caustically.

'Not at all. It was the new arrival,' he said, pointing into the arcade and creasing up with laughter again.

I looked. Sitting just inside the arcade was a big, fluorescent plastic parrot. 'Feed Polly with ten pence and she'll tell your fortune!' said the sign above. The bird opened its mouth and another piercing whistle came out.

I recovered swiftly. 'I *knew* it was the parrot,' I said witheringly. 'I'm not that stupid.'

'Oh yes? Funny – I've never seen anyone looking round and smiling at a plastic parrot before,' he said. 'What was it, the best offer you've had all season?'

42

'Oh, do shut up!' I said as nastily as I could. 'You're quite pathetic.'

He was still laughing as I stalked away. God, I hate him! When I got back to the chalet I pounded my smalls viciously and wished it was his head. How is it that he always manages to get the better of me?

On my way back to carry on Robining later, there was no one (e.g. *him*) around so I went into the arcade and put ten pence into Polly's beak. She gave a loud whistle (and I was expecting it this time) and then swung round and round on a circular disc thing with 'fortunes' written on it and eventually bent down and pecked the one which read: 'You have an admirer in an unexpected quarter.' I looked at the bird stonily; 'Yes, I know, you've already whistled at me,' I muttered as I walked away.

There was a minor riot in the ballroom tonight when one of the day visitors – they're not supposed to be here in the evenings anyway, and certainly aren't allowed to enter the contests – went in for the Knobbly Knee competition and won it.

When Patty took him up on stage so he could do his parading around and showing off his knees bit, there was a rebellious muttering from a couple of the other contestants and then a shout of: 'He's only here for the day! He's not allowed to enter!' from the audience – upon which several men rushed up on stage to thump the judge's table and demand a re-count.

Patty calmed everything down in her usual wonderfully charming way, ('Gentlemen, gentlemen! Is there really any need for this?') then the winner was escorted to the gates with a substitute prize of a glass tankard and a new Knobbly Knees King was announced from the chaps who were left.

Coming back to the chalet at ten o'clock for an early night, I bumped into Mike, real Mike, coming out of the disco.

We smiled at each other; I tried not to faint. 'Hi,' he said.

'I've seen you around quite a bit. You're usually rushing off in the other direction, though.'

I nodded. 'It's pretty hectic.'

'Still enjoying it?'

'It's great,' I said, wondering if the blond streak in his hair could possibly be real, 'it's just that sometimes . . .'

He seemed to know what I was about to say. 'I know, the old place gets a bit on top of you, doesn't it? Perhaps you need a break – how about coming out of the camp for a meal with me some time?'

Managed by sheer effort of will not to fall over backwards, and after we'd fixed day and time (Sunday, main gate at seven-thirty) I wafted back to the chalet in a dream. A date! A real date to make up for Les and the plastic parrot and James and everything . . .

Saturday, 2nd August

It was campers' changeover day so we had quite a bit of free time. This morning Rainbow and I sat outside our chalet in the sun while she compiled a list of Robins' birthdays to see how we should all get on together.

'Do me a favour,' I said, 'don't tell me how I'm going to get on with Mike – let me find it out for myself. I don't want to know if anything's going to go wrong.'

'I'm not working him out,' she said, 'he's not a Robin. Anyway, I don't even know his birthday.'

She carried on making important-looking calculations on pieces of paper. 'Hey, this is surprising,' she said suddenly.

'What is?'

'Seeing as you say you hate him . . .' she muttered. 'Out of all the lot I've done so far, there's someone here you should really get on with.'

'You?' I said.

'Apart from me, of course. Male, I mean.'

44

'Well, they're all OK, I suppose, except for . . .'

'Les!'

'That's who I was going to say.'

She looked up. 'No, I mean *Les* is the one you're compatible with. All the signs are right.'

'But . . . but I can't stand him. He's a pig!' I spluttered.

'That's as may be. I'm just telling you what the stars say,' she said loftily.

I gave a scornful laugh. 'I'd just as soon believe the parrot in the arcade.'

Later on we went over to help ferry the new campers to their chalets and had to put up with the usual cries of: 'Ooh, isn't it small!', 'Ooh, I wanted a blue one!' 'Ooh, I wanted to be nearer the lake/dining room/playground!' etc.

Did notice a group of three really nice-looking boys, all about eighteen or so. Rainbow noticed them, too, and so did Michelle and Emma. It's unusual to get three of them all looking fanciable, even when there's only two, usually one looks like Andrew Ridgeley and the other one looks like Dracula.

Talking of Dracula, I saw Les tonight and he asked me if I'd got a date. Thought he must somehow have heard about me and Mike and I found myself replying quite pleasantly, saying I had.

He looked taken-aback for a moment. 'I meant with your admirer the parrot,' he said.

I narrowed my eyes. So *this* was the person I was supposed to be so compatible with. 'How amusing,' I said, 'I thought you meant was I going out with Mike, the hunky lifeguard, because I am, actually.'

He looked at me coolly. 'Fancy; and I thought you and the parrot were so well-suited,' he said.

I *could* write what I think about him but I'm not sure how to spell the words.

Sunday, 3rd August

Passed the day washing things, writing letters and preparing myself for the date. Rainbow gave my hair a henna conditioning treatment, which consisted of pouring thick wax stuff over it and then slapping hot towels on top for hours on end.

The stuff smelt terrible, got everywhere – and between us we wetted every towel in the place so that when it came to having a shower I had to dry myself on loo paper.

I blow-dried my hair in the tiny hand mirror we've got and then Rainbow stared at me and screwed up her face. 'It looks greasy,' she pronounced. I went over to the window with the mirror and looked more closely: it did. It was so conditioned and contented it was lying there flat to my scalp, zonked out, and I had to wash it all over again.

Finally set off, and on my way to the main gates to meet him, saw Mike II coming towards me wearing an outsize paper hat. As he drew nearer I realised he was also wearing a false nose and glasses – and coming up behind him were a lot of campers, similarly disguised. Hid behind the nappy washing room so he wouldn't see me and they all passed by singing the Birdie Song. It must be some new camp jollity that I haven't heard about.

I nearly fell over when I got to the gates: real Mike looked incredible! I've only ever seen him in swimming trunks or jeans and t-shirt before, but now he was obviously wearing his best going-out-to-dinner outfit: a white suit and underneath, pink shirt with buttons open almost to the waist. He looked like a TV star; I half-expected him to get out a microphone and start singing 'My Way'.

I was only wearing my ordinary red dress and I felt really dowdy next to him; obviously I should have been in a little black and glittery Dallas number. He seemed pleased enough

to see me, though, and we went out of the camp and walked up the main road towards the town.

Was so awe-struck at being with this Barry Manilow lookalike that I forgot my prepared conversation openers. I needn't have worried, though, because he not only opened conversations but also carried them along, finished them and then started new ones all on his own.

'What's a beautiful chick like you doing at Robinson's?' was his first effort, and just as I was opening my mouth to say I wasn't a beautiful chick so he could say I was, he said: 'No, don't answer that.'

I shut my mouth again.

'You're here for the same reason as me, right? To get yourself started in life. To be discovered.'

'Well, I think I . . .'

'You might think I'm just a good-looking muscle man, but I'm a lot more than that, sister!'

Struck dumb at this.

'I mean, Robinson's is just an opening for me, a way into

47

the world of male modelling. I mean to make it to the big time: knitting patterns, home-shopping catalogues – yeah, *really* big.'

Gazed at him open-mouthed.

'I tell you, sooner or later when I'm striding up and down by that pool, someone's going to discover me. I'm going to be Mr Big!'

We were in the restaurant by the time he'd finished telling me all about his ambitions and how he was going to take life by the throat and shake it. He stopped talking long enough to order and then went on to tell me his life history.

'Guess I knew I was special right from the start,' he said modestly. 'Funny, that – how one so young can be so perceptive!'

I murmured something that could have been anything.

'But, well, that's me all over,' he went on, looking at his reflection in the stainless steel water jug and obviously liking what he saw. 'If you've got that little extra something you shouldn't hide it away, that's what I always say. It's just that some guys have it, some guys don't.'

His voice had gone all transatlantic by this time; he sounded just like the sloppy spoken bit you sometimes get on the beginning of records.

'Yeah, right from the time I was four years old and two girls fought over me at nursery school, I knew I wasn't going to have any trouble where birds were concerned.' He smiled in a self-satisfied way, 'Oh, yours truly is always going to have chicks eating out of his hand.'

'You ought to watch out one of them doesn't peck your fingers,' I said, but he was droning on again and didn't hear me, taking me all through primary school (girls tearing their hair out), comprehensive (girls fainting as he walked by) and college (girls lying underfoot in the hopes that he might walk on them). Well, he didn't actually *say* that, but that was the impression I got. Anyway, I may not have heard correctly because I was asleep with my eyes open at the time.

Woke myself up when we got back to the chalet in case he was going to try and kiss me, but he didn't. I don't know whether he was worried about making his suit grubby, didn't think I'd survive being kissed by someone like him, or didn't want to get his lips creased.

Went in stunned, dumbstruck and bored to the point of nausea, and Rainbow fed me a few unwashed sultanas while I tried to recover enough to tell her what had happened.

'You keep being disappointed,' she said when I'd finished, 'perhaps you ought to go where the stars indicate and . . .'

'Don't go on!' I interrupted, 'I've had a terrible enough night as it is!' And I burrowed under my Robin bedspread and wouldn't listen to anything else.

Monday, 4th August

Emma and Michelle came up this morning and said they'd been chatting to the three good-looking boys and they were nice, a real laugh, and just as good-looking close up.

They said they'd arranged to meet them this afternoon in the sports hall and why didn't I come as well?

'I've been talking to Simon mostly and Emma's been talking to Dan,' Michelle said fluffily, 'so it's really Mike who's left out of things so if you . . .'

'*Who*?'

'Mike,' Michelle repeated. 'He's really fun and . . .'

'No thanks!' I said. 'Very kind of you, I'm sure, but no thanks. I've had enough of Mikes. I think I may have Mikeophobia,' I muttered, dashing away.

Had an awful shock just before lunch. I was standing chatting to a couple of pensioners, trying to encourage them to go into the ballroom for Olde Tyme Dancing when someone came up behind me and slipped a hand up the back of my jumper, making me leap about a metre into the air.

'There! I knew I'd catch you without a vest!' said a familiar voice. I wheeled round; it was Mum, of course.

'I said to your dad, I *bet* she's not keeping her kidneys warm.'

'Mum!' I squealed in surprise, giving her a big hug.

'I hope my daughter has been looking after you properly,' Mum beamed at the pensioners.

'Oh, she has, she has!' the old lady said. 'She's been most charming.'

They went off and Dad emerged from behind a hut. 'I told your mother to wait until you were on your own,' he said, 'but she wanted to surprise you.'

'Is Jimmy with you?' I asked eagerly. 'And Richard?'

'We couldn't persuade Richard to come,' Mum said, 'and I wanted to bring Jimmy but when I phoned about coming for the day they said no dogs were allowed. I've had to leave him in the shed.'

'Never mind!' I hugged them both again. 'It's lovely to see you.'

Mum looked round anxiously. 'Now, we don't want to get you into trouble,' she said. 'You mustn't keep talking to us, we'll just walk round behind you and you wave to us when you can.'

'Daft!' I said. 'You won't get me into trouble. I'm here to look after visitors and that's what you are.'

'Only day ones,' Dad said.

'Only day ones still count!'

Had a smashing day – hadn't realised how much I missed them until I saw them. Mum bought me a big home-made fruit cake and a cardboard box full of choccy bars – nearly enough to last me for the rest of my stay. They said that as Dad was on holiday for two weeks and they weren't going away anywhere they might come down again at the end of next week. I told them to bring Jimmy and leave him out in the car; at least I'll be able to go and visit him.

Tuesday, 5th August

'What's all *that*?' Rainbow said in horror this morning, staring at the big fruit cake surrounded by chocolate bars on my bedside table.

'That's a fruit cake,' I said, 'and, let me see, twelve . . . no, thirteen . . .'

'I can see what they are. You're not going to eat them all, are you?'

'No, I thought I'd throw them all up in the air and juggle them.'

'Ha ha,' she said irritably. 'Do you *realise* what you're doing to yourself with all this chocolate rubbish?'

'Yes, thanks!' I found a plastic knife and dug it into the cake. I just fancied a nice slice before breakfast.

'And that cake! Eggs, milk, white flour, sugar!' she said, tapping them off on her fingers, 'and who knows *what* other synthetic poisons!'

'Who knows!' I said happily.

She shook her head. 'It's been nice knowing you.'

Spent the morning avoiding an obnoxious child who's taken it into his head to follow me about. He's about eight, I suppose, with scabby knees and a runny nose. He's one of last Saturday's arrivals and I felt a bit sorry for him at first – he seems to be an only child and his parents are quite old. Made the fatal mistake of making a bit of a fuss of him yesterday afternoon (I was showing off to Mum and Dad, actually) and since then he's dogged my footsteps, asking embarrassing questions with every step.

The questions mostly concern me and are of the: 'Have you got a boyfriend?' 'Does he kiss you?' variety. It was a novelty at first, rather sweet, I thought, but when it got to this afternoon and he was still there, standing outside the staff canteen waving at me with runny nose pressed on the glass, I began to get a bit ratty.

'You certainly attract quite a following,' Les said, nodding towards the window. 'Nine year olds, plastic parrots – no stopping you, is there?'

Gave him a glower. He always makes me so cross that I go all speechless.

The Child followed me round until four o'clock when I managed to lose him in Auntie Bertie's Magic Rabbit Show, and then he reappeared and stuck to me all the time I was trying to take names for the children's races.

When his parents came up he'd just asked me to mind a half-chewed piece of gum for him and I'd just pretended I couldn't hear him.

'So nice of you to keep our boysie amused,' they said. 'He's taken a real liking to you.'

'Has he ... er ... really?' I said, patting him on the head quite hard. 'Such a nice little boy.'

'We wanted to go out this evening and we wondered if you'd babysit for us. Could you come to our chalet?' his

mother asked. She was thin, intense, and was wearing a dress made out of something like curtain material.

'I'm really sorry,' I lied, 'I'm not allowed to. You'll have to get one of the nursery nurses to listen in.'

'Oh dear, boysie was so looking forward to it,' his mother said fondly. 'Never mind, he'll have to see his Auntie Robin tomorrow.'

Gave him another pat and mumbled that I'd have to go. Broke into a run and managed to shake him off somewhere between the amusement arcade and the hamburger bar.

Popped into the disco this evening but saw immediately that they didn't need anyone to get things going; Emma was already there, had the microphone in an iron grip and was levering people on to the dance floor.

'Come along now, not enough boys are dancing!' she boomed. 'I want everyone – and I mean everyone – to find themselves a partner and get moving.'

53

I watched as everyone shuffled uneasily. 'Well now, boys, if you can't find yourselves a partner we'd better have a Ladies Excuse-Me,' she ordered. 'Let's have all the girls lined up here . . . right here, please, come along!'

I crept away quietly. Funny, she seems quite OK when she's on her own, but show her a couple of campers and she jumps into action. They *will* have a good time, or she'll know the reason why.

When I got back to the chalet Rainbow was already in bed with a bedcover over her head.

'Whatever's up?' I said. 'Don't you feel well?'

'No. I've got a cold,' she sniffed.

'Ha! It's all that stuff you eat!' I said triumphantly. 'Those greens and beans and nuts are no good for you. What you need is a nice juicy steak.'

She lowered the cover a little; her eyes were blotchy, her nose pink. I stared at her in dismay. 'It's not a cold, is it? You've been crying!'

She burst into tears and wiped her nose on the bedcover.

'It's Kevin. We've had an awful row,' she sniffed. 'I told him he was a blood-thirsty vampire and I didn't want to see him again.'

'Oh dear,' I said, still staring. I hoped I wasn't going to laugh but she looked so funny sitting up there with a red nose, black-smudged eyes, the bedcover over her head and her mouth all covered with . . .

'Chocolate!' I shouted suddenly. 'You've got chocolate all over your face!'

'Have I?' she asked in a small voice.

'You know you have!' I turned suddenly and looked at my goody pile – it was about six bars smaller. 'You've been eating my chocolate!'

She burst out crying again. 'I know! I couldn't help it! It's only when I'm feeling a bit miserable and I was feeling *very* miserable and I just tried a piece to cheer me up and then I

54

tried a piece more and before I knew it . . .' she pushed aside the pillow to reveal a big pile of coloured wrappers and silver foil. 'I'll buy you another lot tomorrow, really I will. I just couldn't help it . . .'

'It's not *that*,' I managed to say, 'it's . . . I mean, you're so *anti* stuff like chocolate, so sarcastic when I eat it. You go on and on at me and. . . .'

'I know. It's because I like it so much. I'm like a . . . a chocoholic! I have to stay away from junk food or I can't stop eating it.'

I began to giggle in spite of the seriousness of the occasion. 'It's not the first time you've lapsed, is it?'

She shook her head sadly. 'I'm just an out and out hypocrite. I ate some of your toffees and some fruit and nut and some of your packet of brandy snaps – oh, and a big blob of cream you left on a box lid.'

'You do realise,' I said, 'that you'll never be able to say anything to me again about junk food, never be able to tell me that I'm poisoning my system or ruining my body?'

She shook her head sadly. 'Never again. And I'm sorry. But . . . but what shall I do about Kevin?'

'I'll try and see him and chat to him, if you like,' I offered. I reached for a Mars bar. 'Want another one of these?'

'No thanks. I feel sick,' she said woefully.

Wednesday, 6th August

A mopey sort of day; felt I couldn't much care whether the campers lived or died. Rainbow flopped around looking distraught and red-eyed and her mood must have affected me because I came over all fed up, too.

Boys are a dead loss. Rainbow's fallen out with Kevin and I thought I'd have had millions of holiday romances by now and I haven't had one.

Tonight Les said that the two of us looked like a rainbow

55

with an accompanying raincloud. Felt too fed up to retaliate. Or to write any more now.

Thursday, 7th August

Things have brightened up a bit today, mostly due to a talk this morning from Patty about putting our best faces forward – I think she must have seen Rainbow and me drooping about looking like dead Robins yesterday.

'Now, I'm not mentioning any names,' she said brightly, when we'd assembled in the Nest, 'but it's come to my attention that *some* of my newer Robins aren't exactly doing their chirrupy best!'

I kicked Rainbow and she kicked me back.

'You must realise,' Patty went on, 'that how a Robin behaves can affect the whole camp. I mean, don't we want our campers to have happy holidays?'

No one replied so she said again,

'I said, don't we *want* our campers to have happy holidays?' and replied enthusiastically for herself, 'Oh, of *course* we do!'

'Do we?' I heard muttered beside me.

'So let's all practise our big smiles and go out of here ready to make everyone feel ON TOP OF THE WORLD!' she shouted, making everyone jump.

She looked at us critically. 'I think what we all could do with are some smiling exercises! We all need these sometimes to remind our faces how it's done!' While we watched, dumbstruck, she contorted her lips into a great pout and said: 'Ooooh!' then stretched them sideways almost to her ears: 'Eeeeeh!'

'Copy me!' she commanded. 'Ooooh.... Eeeeeh.... Ooooh.... Eeeeh ...'

From beside me there was a muffled snort of laughter, but I oooohed and eeeehed along with everyone else; I didn't dare turn round in case I had hysterics.

'There!' Patty said at last. 'Doesn't that feel good? You've got those old smile muscles working a treat!' She punched her fist into the air, 'Now, let's get out there and use them!' She gave a final triumphant 'Whee!' and marched out of the door.

There was a moment's stunned silence and then everyone burst out laughing and couldn't stop.

I saw Kevin later and had a cosy chat with him. I said that Rainbow was very miserable and hadn't meant half the things she'd said, and if he wanted to make it up he could come to the chalet tonight with a large bar of chocolate.

He looked at me in amazement. 'She hates chocolate!' he said.

I winked. 'That's what you think.'

This afternoon I spent a couple of hours helping out in the shoe shop. Most of my time was taken up helping one woman choose a pair of flip-flops; first of all she had the various colours spread out in front of her: blue, green, red, yellow, then once we'd gone through her entire holiday wardrobe to see which colour would go best with everything and decided on blue, we had a very long debate on whether the sole of the blue flip-flop wasn't a little harder than the others.

'The red one feels a lot softer, somehow,' she said worriedly, 'and I do rather suffer with my feet.'

When she'd changed to red, tried them on and walked up and down the shop a few times, she then said they were hurting her just between her toes and she wondered if she ought to try the yellow. Eventually she came down in favour of green because in her size it was just a fraction shorter than the other colours, and she didn't want to trip up. Could cheerfully have flip-flopped her round the head; it was only the thought of the pep talk from Patty that kept me from doing so.

Rainbow was all smiles when she came in this evening;

57

she and Kevin had made it up *and* she'd confessed to him about being a chocoholic and everything.

It would be nice if I could find someone now. Just a small, modest sort of holiday romance doesn't seem much to ask . . .

Friday, 8th August

Got up early and sent a pile of postcards to various friends and relations at home.

Bumped into Mike I when I was coming out of breakfast; he was wearing a white silk dressing gown affair with his initials on it and he looked at me as if he thought he knew me vaguely but wasn't quite sure about it. Funny, I should have seen from the start what he was: he doesn't actually wear one, but he's obviously an *undercover medallion man*.

About eleven o'clock things suddenly began to look up. I became aware that Someone was looking at me: a visitor I'd never seen before, a good-looking one with longish fair hair and very dark eyes.

'Excuse me,' he said, coming up. 'You're a Robin, aren't you?'

'I certainly am,' I said, putting on one of my best Patty look-alike smiles. 'How can I help you?'

'Well, how about coming out with me tonight? Or is that against the rules?'

Flummox . . . flummox . . . 'Er, no,' I gulped.

'No, you won't come out with me or no, it's not against the rules?'

'It's not against the rules,' I said, looking dazedly into his eyes. Talk about a fast worker.

'It might seem a bit sudden but I've been watching you flitting about and I thought if I didn't say something soon, you might disappear into the masses.'

'And never be seen again . . .'

'Exactly,' he said. We smiled at each other. I felt all funny inside: as if I'd eaten six Mars bars.

'I'm officially on duty tonight,' I said, 'but as long as I stay on the camp it's all right, I can more or less go where I want to.'

'Great,' he said. 'We could go to the cinema, then, or have a meal or something?'

'Whatever you like.'

'So, I'll meet you somewhere – by the amusement arcade, say? About seven-thirty?'

I nodded. 'Though I expect I'll be seeing you around all day now.'

I gave him another Patty-type sparkler and walked away bestowing gentle smiles on everyone I passed. Once out of his sight I galloped around until I found Rainbow.

'This is IT,' I said excitedly. 'The Holiday Romance. It's

going to be all moonlit walks along the shore and gazing into each other's eyes under the palm trees. Straight out of Mills and Boon.'

'We're a bit short of exotic locations round here,' she said. 'You'll have to be satisfied with walking under the fluorescent strip lighting and gazing into his eyes over a space invader machine.'

It's now seven-fifteen; I've ditched my evening meal to have more time to make myself devastating, and am now sitting by our chalet window dowsed in Rainbow's musk oil ('It never fails') perfume and waiting to go.

Later

It's nine-fifteen and I'm having an early night with two bars of chocolate.

He didn't turn up. I waited and waited, skirting round the amusement arcade, staring with great interest at the fruit machines and the plastic parrot and looking at my watch every two seconds.

At eight o'clock I'd just about decided to go, when Les appeared. I turned my back and pretended to wave to someone further in the arcade, but he came up to me.

'What's up? Been left in the lurch?' he said cheerfully.

I gave him a Horrible Look. 'None of your business.'

'I just wondered. Only, that guy I saw you chatting to this morning . . .'

I spun round, unable to resist asking. 'What about him?'

'He was a day visitor. When they sounded the bell he left with a crowd of others.'

I stared at him and to my horror felt tears coming into my eyes. 'And aren't you pleased to be the one to come up and tell me!' I burst out angrily. 'That's just about made your day, hasn't it?'

Before he could say anything else I pushed past him and ran away, sniffing and snuffling noisily. Why was it *him* who had to tell me? I hate him. And I hate *him*, this morning – have just realised that I don't even know his name. Fancy making a date like that when he knew he wouldn't be here; he must have done it just for a laugh.

That's *it* now. No more dates; I've had it with boys. I'm going to go in for lots of face-stretching exercises and devote myself to helping people have a wonderful holiday; I'm going to be a Super-Robin. When I've had a good cry, that is.

Saturday, 9th August

Felt a bit fed up first thing this morning, thinking of all the relationships that have hit the dust (or not even got up out of it in the first place) over the past weeks, including James, but then I remembered about being a Super-Robin and I fluffed up my feathers a bit and got going.

A funny thing happened just before lunch: Les came wandering up to me as I was cutting across the football pitch on my way to the staff canteen. I thought he was going to say something sarcastic to me, as usual, so I turned a king-size glower at him, all ready for it. Nearly collapsed in a heap when he gave me a funny lop-sided smile and said: 'I think I ought to say sorry to you.'

'What . . . what d'you mean?' I gulped.

'Well, yesterday. I didn't mean to upset you, telling you about that guy leaving camp.'

'It's OK,' I muttered, completely taken-aback. 'It didn't matter.'

'It did though, didn't it?' he insisted. 'I felt rotten when you rushed away. I could see you were upset.'

I looked at him closely; he seemed to mean it – his ears had even gone pink round the edges.

'I reckon – well, when I thought about it after, I reckon the guy didn't know he was going to have to go at six o'clock. He looked dead surprised to find himself leaving so early.'

61

'*Did* he?' I felt a bit consoled. Maybe I hadn't been deliberately stood up after all.

Les nodded. 'Honest.' He hesitated and I didn't know whether to carry on walking or not. 'Look,' he said suddenly, 'we got off to a pretty bad start, didn't we?'

'You could say that.'

'I was in a rotten mood that first day. And since then, well, you seem to take everything I say the wrong way, when half the time I don't really mean it.'

'Don't you?' I asked squeakily, not knowing where to look.

'Every time you see me your hackles go up. You expect me to have a go at you, don't you, and then I can't resist doing it.'

'Oh,' I said. I was really getting confused: one minute he was my sworn enemy, the next we were having a heart-to-heart.

'It's a bit like when I tease my kid sister. Nothing nasty meant.'

I looked somewhere just beyond his pink right ear. 'I see,' I said. 'I think.' I shuffled my feet. 'Anyway, I'd better go.'

'And Janey,'

'Yes?'

'It's true what someone once said: you only tease people you like.'

'Oh,' I said again. I glanced into his eyes, just for a moment, and glanced away again quickly. He was looking at me too intently, too seriously, and it took me back to the first day before I'd realised what a pig he was. Well, he was, wasn't he?

'Friends?' he asked, holding out his hand.

'Well, OK,' I said. I touched his hand briefly, mumbled that I *had* to go and ran for it. It was all too bewildering.

This afternoon I found it difficult to concentrate on what I was doing; I kept taking new people from Reception to the wrong chalets.

'What's up with you?' Rainbow asked, catching up with me as we walked back to the main hall together. 'You're all of a dither.'

'I've had a funny conversation with Les,' I said. 'Most peculiar.'

'What, more sarcasm at your expense, was it?'

'No,' I said, 'that's just it. He was actually serious. I think.'

'Mmm, I'm not surprised,' Rainbow said reflectively. 'I think all that messing about is just a cover and he's not really like that at all.'

'Not really a big-headed, self-opinionated pig?'

'No,' she said. 'His rising sign is Gemini, see, so he . . .'

'Don't start on all that again!' I said, preparing to swoop on a couple trying to get through Reception without registering. 'I don't believe a word of it!'

Helped out at Bingo tonight. They let me pick out the coloured balls and I tried to make an old lady win by keeping a couple of balls back instead of calling them out. Got into a terrible muddle and in the end I had to drop the balls on the floor, say: 'Oops, I *am* clumsy!' and start the whole game again. Don't suppose she even *wanted* a fluffy pink nightdress case shaped like a rabbit and saying 'You're no bunny until some bunny loves you' anyway.

Sunday, 10th August

There's a whole new campful of people – with just about ten staying over from the week before. On Sunday mornings it's funny to see all the new ones roaming about in packs clutching their little paper maps and trying to get their bearings.

As it was our day off we slept in late (or tried to sleep with what seemed like two million people trooping past) and then Rainbow got up and washed her hair and I did it in hundreds of little plaits with beads on the end. Well, it should have been hundreds of little plaits but I didn't have much patience and my arms ached after about ten, so she ended up with about twenty-five and it didn't look quite right.

This afternoon we were sitting sunning ourselves outside the chalet when Patty came up and said would I mind awfully, but they had a honeymoon couple arriving at Reception at four o'clock and it would be *so* helpful if I could find a moment to check that the Executive Chalet was ready, then go and collect them and escort them to it.

'If you go and see the catering manager, he's got a wedding pack ready for you,' she said mysteriously as I set off.

Went into the kitchens and found the manager asleep with a Sunday paper over his face, which he lifted briefly to nod towards a box in the corner. I looked in, it contained a bottle of champàgne with ice bucket and two glasses, a box of chocolates and a bowl of fruit. Found out later that Robinson's don't get many honeymoon couples (I'm not surprised), so when they do get them, they make a fuss of them.

Took the box over to our Executive Chalet. There are two of these, they keep them for when Mr Robinson himself visits the camp or for visiting dignitaries and VIPs. They're about twice as big as the ordinary ones, with their own sitting room, hallway and posh bathroom. They also have fitted carpets, colour TV and framed photographs of Robinsons Through the Ages on the walls.

We get very few people who arrive other than on a Saturday afternoon, so when I went over to Reception it was almost deserted apart from a few children sliding about on the tiled floor.

I spotted the honeymoon couple straight away; they were both wearing brand new going-away clothes and were standing very close to each other and talking intimately, looking into each other's eyes. Felt quite soppy when I saw them.

'Hello!' I gushed in a voice dripping with Patty-style friendliness, 'Welcome to Robinson's!'

'Well, thanks,' the guy said, running a finger round inside his collar nervously.

'I've come to take you to your special chalet and make sure you've got everything you need,' I said.

The girl smiled and didn't say anything. *He* said: 'We've got a . . . er . . . special chalet?'

'At Robinson's we like to give you that little extra attention,' I beamed, going flat out for the Golden Feather award.

I carried one of their cases and led the way to the Executive Chalet, chatting all the way about the activities they could join in and all the things there were to do in the evenings – then I remembered they were there on honeymoon and shut up.

I flung open the chalet door dramatically. 'I *do* hope you'll be happy here!' I cried, putting the case down.

'Champagne!' I heard the girl say as I made a discreet exit. 'I don't quite believe this!'

'Must be some new promotion or something,' the guy said, 'the chalets didn't look like this in the brochure.'

Went back to tell Patty that all had gone well and they were safely installed.

'I knew I could rely on you,' she said fondly, and I went back to my own chalet feeling not only a super-Robin, but a right crawler.

Monday, 11th August

Saw my honeymoon couple on my way to breakfast.

'I hope you were pleased with everything,' I said, and then realised too late how that must have sounded, and went red.

'Everything was fine,' the guy said, 'and I must say I've never had such super treatment at a holiday camp ever before. I'll definitely be coming back here again!'

Smiled modestly, as if I'd personally paid for the champagne, fruit and chocolates. 'That's Robinson's for you,' I said, 'we do try and . . .'

'I mean, Peter and I might never have got together if it hadn't been for you,' the girl said shyly.

'You met here last year?'

'Last night!' the guy said.

I stopped dead in my tracks. I must have heard wrong. 'Last night?' I asked in a baffled voice.

'Yesterday in your reception. We were just chatting . . .' here the girl looked up at him adoringly, 'I was telling Peter that my friend had let me down and I was here on my own and he was sympathising.'

'And then *you* appeared and ushered us off to champagne and everything. Like some sort of dating service, it was,' the guy beamed.

'But . . . but . . . you're not the honeymoon couple?' I asked faintly.

66

He roared with laughter. 'That's a good one! I never set eyes on Avril until yesterday.'

The girl laughed softly. 'And it's all due to you that we're a real couple now.'

I stared from one to the other. 'Oh dear,' I said faintly.

'It's a great idea of Robinson's, though. What a start to a relationship!'

I opened my mouth to say 'Oh dear' again but nothing came out.

'See you later!' they said cheerfully, and walked off hand in hand, leaving me standing there.

Les was the first person I saw. I was going to make a bolt for it but then I remembered we were friends now, sort of, and I stumbled up and told him in a strangled voice what I'd done. 'They didn't even know each other,' I kept repeating. 'I put them in the Executive Chalet and they didn't even *know* each other . . .'

He couldn't stop laughing. I shook his arm urgently. 'What shall I do, though? Shall I ask them to move out? Where d'you think the real honeymoon couple are?'

'You'd better go and see Patty straight after breakfast,' he said when he'd stopped laughing. 'She'll sort it all out.'

In the end Patty saw me before I'd even got to the canteen.

'Whatever's happened?!' she said. 'I saw Mr and Mrs Jenkins – the honeymoon couple – coming out of an ordinary chalet, and when I asked them if they'd enjoyed the champagne they looked at me as if I was mad.'

I hung my head, mentally said goodbye to the Golden Feather award and told all. Later on the real honeymoon couple were moved into the other Executive Chalet and given another wedding pack.

It's been all right actually; it seems that everyone, even Patty, has seen the funny side of it. Word has got all over camp and this afternoon other Robins were coming up to me and saying things like: 'Could you fix me up with a tall guy and have him delivered to my chalet at five-thirty with a bottle of champagne, please.'

Les keeps cracking jokes about me but I'm not getting ratty. I'm glad we're friends. Before I had to be on my guard all the time, now it's so much easier.

Tuesday, 12th August

Mum, Dad, Richard and Jimmy came down today. This morning I wasn't sure if it *was* Richard – he spent the entire time huddled into a jacket with the collar turned right up in case anyone he knew saw him in a holiday camp, but this afternoon he relaxed a bit and, while Mum and Dad played a game of bowls, he went for a swim and then we walked round together and he told me all the happenings at home. Well, some of them, anyway; boys don't seem to be much good at bits of gossip; things go on right under their noses and they never actually notice.

I saw Les twice. The first time he looked as if he was going to come up and speak, then he saw Richard and seemed to change his mind. The second time he pretended he hadn't seen me, but I know he had.

Don't exactly know how I feel about him now. I was instantly attracted to him that first day, then decided I hated him – couldn't *stand* him – but since that talk my feelings have been all muddled. I think of the things he's said to me over the weeks and feel I could kill him, and then I think of him all embarrassed and pink-eared and everything gets mixed up. Do I like him, or don't I? And what sort of like is it? What I keep wondering is, if the first chalet mix-up hadn't happened and we'd started off as friends, where would we be now?

Forgot to say how *lovely* it was to see Jimmy. He had to stay out in the car park, of course, but I made lots of trips to see him and he practically licked me to death each time.

When Mum and everyone had gone, I wandered off to the ballroom to see what was going on and found the Miss Party Girl contest in full swing. It wasn't quite as embarrassing as the Fat 'n' Fun, but almost: each woman, (none of them were exactly girls) had to go up on stage on her own and tell a funny story, sing a song or recite a poem.

One of them had come all prepared with a lurex dress and a songsheet. She sang 'I belong to Glasgow', 'Maybe it's because I'm a Londoner' and 'When Irish eyes are Smiling' straight off before anyone could stop her, pausing only to say she hoped none of the judges were Welsh because she didn't know a Welsh song.

The next one said she didn't know any proper poems but she recited 'Mary had a little lamb' and did a funny sort of dance. The third one said she didn't know any funny stories, couldn't remember a poem and wouldn't dream of singing in public.

'Right!' the compère said. 'Which film star or personality would you most like to meet?'

The woman thought for a moment and then said Tarzan. 'Well, it so happens,' the compère said immediately, 'that we've got Tarzan right here tonight!' He winked at one of the male Robins backstage and he took his jumper and shirt off. 'This must be your lucky day, Mrs Maythorpe!'

Mrs Maythorpe was told to go and stand on one of the little tables surrounding the dance floor (the people sitting at it just sat there dumbfounded) and then Tarzan came in making loud Tarzan noises and thumping his chest.

Mrs Maythorpe shrieked, the audience had hysterics and Tarzan swung her over his shoulder and carried her off backstage.

I'm not sure what it all had to do with being Miss Party Girl but the audience seemed to like it. Whenever one of the women couldn't do a turn, the compère asked her who she'd like to meet and then one of the Robins would pretend to be him. We had Superman, Paul Newman, Rudolph Nureyev and Jimmy Young there tonight.

Walked back afterwards with Michelle. She and Emma spent nearly all week with that Simon and Dan they met, and since they've been home they've all been writing to each other. Maybe I should have risked it. Third Mike lucky and all that.

Wednesday, 13th August

A camper knocked loudly on her window as I was passing through the long row of blue chalets this morning.

'Young lady,' she called, flinging the window open and nearly hitting me on the nose, 'there are rats in these chalets!'

'What?' I said.

'Rats. I can distinctly hear them scrabbling about at night.'

'Oh, I'm sure you're mistaken,' I said, thoughts of Bubonic Plague and the Black Death running through my head. 'Shall I come in and . . . er . . . listen?'

I went in and put my ear to her floorboards but couldn't hear a thing. 'Of course, they're quiet *now* because they know we're on to them,' she said.

I promised I'd tell the Accommodation Manager – and meanwhile marked her off as a bit batty – and promptly forgot about her.

This afternoon I was over on the field watching Emma force children to have donkey rides when a little girl came up and asked me where you could buy seed.

'Seed?' I said, baffled.

'You see, I want to take some home as a present,' she said earnestly. 'It's for my gerbil.'

I shook my head. 'I don't think you'll find going-home presents for gerbils in any of the camp shops,' I said, 'you'll have to get Mum or Dad to take you to a pet shop outside.'

'But I don't want them to know,' she said worriedly. 'Perhaps he'll eat bread.'

Didn't put these two strange incidents together, until I passed along the blue chalets again later and saw the same little girl playing with something in the long grass next to the 'ratty' chalet.

'Hi,' I said. 'Who are you talking to?'

71

'Fairies,' she said promptly, putting something behind her back.

It was then that I fell in. 'Have you got your gerbil here on holiday with you?' I asked.

'No,' she said, then 'Ow! He bit me!'

It turned out that she hadn't been able to find anyone at home to mind her gerbil while she was away, so her mum had told her she'd have to take it back to the shop. She hadn't wanted to do this, of course, so she'd smuggled the gerbil away in a cardboard box inside her suitcase. She'd been letting it out for a run in the evenings while her mum and dad were at the camp theatre or wherever; that's why the woman in the next chalet had heard little feet scrabbling about.

I made her promise to look after 'Gerry' carefully and not to let him get away, and then I went and helped myself to some of Rainbow's sunflower seeds; I knew she wouldn't mind. Suppose I really should have reported it to some camp official, but I didn't want to get the little girl into trouble.

After supper tonight I went over to the ballroom and had a few quicksteps round the floor with some old chaps in beige cardigans and braces. Well, *they* quickstepped, I shuffled my feet around very quickly and tried to keep them from being trodden on.

Coming back at eleven o'clock I found Rainbow standing in the chalet doorway looking bemused.

'What's up?' I asked. 'Why aren't you going in?'

'Because someone's in your bed, that's why.'

'What?!'

'Look!' she pointed.

I looked. From the light filtering through the Robin curtains a tall shape could be seen in my bed, nestling under my bedcover.

'I knew it wasn't you,' she said in a hoarse whisper. 'I *knew* something was wrong.'

'You read it in the stars?' I asked faintly.

'No, I asked you if you wanted a chocolate cream egg and you didn't reply.'

'Is he . . . breathing?'

We both held our breath and listened, but there was so much noise from people outside going by that we couldn't tell.

'You don't think . . .'

'What if he's dead . . .' we both said at the same time, and backed away.

'You keep watch, I'll go and get Kevin,' Rainbow said.

'That's OK, *I'll* go and get Kevin.'

'Look, you wait outside,' she said. 'We don't want him to escape, do we?'

'I don't mind if he does,' I said in a plaintive voice. 'I'd rather he escaped than hid in my bed all night.' But she was gone, sprinting down the line of staff chalets.

I stood there, breath bated, and after a moment she came back with Kevin, armed with a saucepan. We all stared at each other.

'Shall I get Security?' I whispered.

'No, let's find out who it is first,' Kevin said. 'You pull the bedclothes back and I'll get ready to hit him over the head with the saucepan.'

'Not too hard,' Rainbow put in nervously.

On the edge of hysterics, we tiptoed in. I took a deep breath, pulled back the bedspread – and almost collapsed with shock.

Lying peacefully, its head resting on my pillow, was a large brown plastic alligator; one of the animals from the island on the boating lake. It lay right along the length of the bed with mouth agape and teeth gleaming, its shiny brown feet to each side of the mattress as if trying it for size.

Rainbow and I clutched each other and started to giggle. It was all we could do, really.

Wonder who put it there? More to the point, wonder what we can do to get back at whoever-it-is when we know?

73

Thursday, 14th August

Quite a few people knew about the alligator, they were all laughing when Rainbow and I went into breakfast. No one would say how they knew, or who put it there, though. Bet it was Les.

We rowed across to the island straight after breakfast to return it, and had a good look at the other animals while we were there to see what we can get off easily when we've discovered who the joker is. I thought it would be rather nice to have a hippo and put it in someone's shower, but Rainbow said it was too big and hefty to handle properly.

This afternoon someone pointed out the real honeymoon couple to me; they were walking hand in hand through the table tennis room. Must say I'd never have picked them for a honeymoon couple; they're quite old, for a start, and he had a big bushy beard and was wearing baggy jeans which hung down at the back and revealed a small piece of his bottom. Wouldn't fancy going on honeymoon with *him*.

Saw the fake ones today, too. Feel dead embarrassed when I think about that; fancy them not saying they'd only just met, though.

Les was in the fairground later and I decided to go up and tackle him about the alligator and see if I could catch him out, but when I got closer I saw he was chatting up a girl.

Felt quite awkward. Dodged behind a crowd of children so he wouldn't see me and managed to get out round the back of the helter-skelter.

Wondered who she was all afternoon and then I saw them again when I was going into the children's theatre with Emma.

'See Les has found himself a girlfriend, then,' I said casually. 'Who is she – a day visitor?'

Emma craned her neck to look. 'No, she's one of the nursery nurses,' she said, 'it must be her day off.'

'Oh,' I said, and suddenly I felt all miserable and devastated and didn't know why.

At suppertime Patty said that someone from the press office was bringing over a reporter from a national paper tomorrow.

'We want to show them what fun a holiday camp is,' she said, 'but also how up-to-date. It's not like *Hi-de-Hi* any more, we like to feel we've moved with the times, so I want you to try and keep him away from the Knobbly Knee Contest and the . . . er . . . grotty chalets and show him the tennis courts, gymnasium and the new chalets with their own loo.'

'There's one more thing,' she finished, after giving us a long list of where she wanted him to go and where she didn't, 'we've had a memo from Mr Robinson' – she almost curtseyed when she said his name – 'and he's requested that we don't call ourselves a holiday *camp* any more, but a holiday centre. And the campers aren't to be campers.'

'What are they going to be, then?' someone asked.

'Visitors,' she said. 'Holidaymakers, guests ... anything but campers. We want to go up-market.'

- Hope I don't get lumbered with showing the reporter round; I'm bound to show him all the wrong things.

Friday, 15th August

Was stopped by small, very pleasant woman this morning who wanted to know the way to the indoor swimming pool. As we were several blocks from it I walked over there with her – she chatting all the way about what a very pleasant place it was and wanting to know how I liked being a Robin.

'I do admire you all – it must be very hard work,' she said.

I nodded. 'We get some really awkward people to deal with, too,' I said confidingly, 'but whatever they're like, even if they're really insulting, we still have to be nice to them.'

'I suppose you do,' she agreed. 'I haven't seen a Robin so far who hasn't been smiling.'

'That's probably because we get it drilled into us a million times a day,' I said. 'That – and our smiling exercises. Stretch ... pout ... stretch ... pout ...' I went through a few of Patty's faces for her. 'We actually had to *do* this last week!'

'Amazing!' she said, laughing.

'Not that there isn't plenty to smile at anyway – what with the Fat 'n' Fun Competition and the Miss Party Girl and the Lowest Limbo Competition!'

'What are all those?'

Explained briefly and did a quick demonstration limbo for her, then left her outside the swimming pool. Wondered afterwards how it was that she didn't know where it was – and why she hadn't heard of any of the competitions when it was Friday and she must have been there a week, but flung myself bodily into helping with the children's gymnastics competition and thought no more about it.

Patty came to the staff canteen at lunchtime wearing six inches of lip gloss and accompanied by a tall man carrying a tape recorder and camera. Ah ha, I thought, the reporter.

'This is Sam Meadows,' she said to the little crowd of us Robins on the bottom table, 'he's the photographer with Alice Newman, the reporter I told you about.'

She looked around, and two tables down Alice Newman got up and waved at us – the small woman I'd taken to the swimming pool, of course – and made laugh about the smiling exercises and the state of the competitions. Wonder if it'll make the Nationals? If Patty finds out it was me who told her I expect I'll be unfeathered.

This afternoon the camp – sorry, centre – was as it usually is on a Friday; full of people exchanging addresses, promising to send Christmas cards to each other and swearing eternal friendship. A lot of photographs were taken, too, and as they always want a pet Robin smiling out cheerfully from the centre, I got called upon a few times. Funny to think of me on mantelpieces all round the country: 'Who's *that* with the big false smile and the red woolly?' 'Oh, that's just one of the Robins.'

Found out Les's nursery nurse is called Lulu. How can he possibly like anyone called Lulu? Found out her date of birth, too, by devious means, and asked Rainbow how suitable she is for Les (just interested for the sake of astrological science, of course).

Rainbow loves being taken seriously and asked things like that; she immediately got all her books off the shelf, started riffling through the pages and muttering things to herself.

'No,' she said eventually, 'they're not suited.'

'No? What else? What about all that stuff you've been poring over?'

She frowned. 'It's very technical for the unenlightened.'

'Yes, but . . . *why* is it no?'

'Because she's got Mars on the ascendant, he's got his moon in Virgo and because I say so.'

Saturday, 16th August

The usual sort of changeover day: the place was a seething mass of people scurrying about with cases, shouting to each other and tripping over children until eleven o'clock, then it was drastically quiet for a couple of hours, then a whole new mass of people began scurrying about again.

We were on Reception duty as usual this afternoon ('Now, Robins, keep those smiles right out front!') and by four o'clock my cheeks ached so much I reckon I felt like the Queen must feel after receiving two million people at one of her Do's.

One thing, at least I had a glimpse of two new boys: Jeff and Dave, they arrived about three o'clock and had jokingly asked me for a date by three-fifteen.

Laughingly declined, whilst doing all possible to let them (or Jeff, at least) know I might be interested if he asked me properly.

Going towards the canteen at about five-thirty I noticed two girls sitting on the grass sort-of draped all over each other and shrieking. Thought at first one of them might be crying and the other one comforting her, so went up and asked if there was anything I could do.

They stared at me for a moment, startled: they looked pretty much alike, sixteenish, both wearing jeans, one dark and one mousey-haired, then they collapsed into what I then realised was hysterics of giggles again.

I felt like hearing something funny so I sat down on the grass next to them and handed over the paper hanky that a good Robin always has folded up her sleeve for emergencies.

'It was Tina – trying on jeans!' the mousey one managed to say after a while, and then I had to wait until they'd both collapsed again and got over it.

At last Tina managed to speak. 'We've been in the boutique,' she said shakily. 'I wanted some really tight jeans so I tried on a stretch pair that were a size too small.'

'Yes?' I said encouragingly.

'Well, we were in this really tiny fitting room with just a curtain right round, and all of a sudden they said they were about to close the shop, so I panicked a bit.'

'And got stuck in them?' I asked.

They exchanged further giggles. 'Just for a while,' Tina said then, 'but Lyn pulled me out. It wasn't *that* . . .'

'What then?'

This time I had to wait a couple of minutes. I found myself giggling along with them, even though I didn't have the faintest idea what it was all about.

'It's . . . it's her knickers!' Lyn burst out suddenly. 'She's just discovered that in the panic she's left her knickers inside the stretch jeans!'

'They were new for the holiday, too,' Tina said. 'Pink lace with white bows. I'll never *dare* get them back.'

Was going to go in the shop myself when I'd finished laughing, but the boutique was closed – and anyway, I don't know if my duties extend to rescuing other people's knickers from stretch jeans.

Sat near Les in the canteen tonight. Think he'd just washed his hair because it looked all shiny and soft and I almost had to sit on my hands so I wouldn't try to touch it. I sound like a shampoo advertisement but I'm getting a bit worried; I think I really like him. In a way I reckon it would have been better if he'd carried on being awful to me. Things were much less complicated then – I hated him and that was that.

Sunday, 17th August

Les was with Lulu in the breakfast queue this morning. Made myself go up and chat to them in an extremely friendly way, even though I'd have liked to push her nose in the porridge.

Had a real good look at her. She has gingery hair and lots of freckles and very pale blue eyes. Quite attractive, I suppose, if you like that type. She's a bit sweet, though, and I've noticed her doing sickly things like patting children fondly on the head as they go by. I can just picture her in the nursery with children clambering all over her, being soft and fluffy and not saying 'For God's sake, will you leave me *alone*!' like I would.

Back to the chalet after breakfast to make a vague attempt to clear things up a bit and write some letters home. Managed a very long one to Anna telling her all about Les and asking her advice, but knowing her she won't get round to replying until I'm home again.

Asked Rainbow twice if she was quite sure that Les and Lulu were incompatible ('Not again! I've told you loads of times they're not!') and then painted a lot of pale brown freckles over my nose to see what they looked like.

Couldn't get quite the right effect, somehow, so I wiped them off and then walked round the *centre* (I remembered) to look for Jeff and Dave. Found them playing tennis and sat for a while being a bright and entertaining Robin while they got their breath back.

Have decided I might forego being a Super-Robin and go out with Jeff if he asks. Well, I might as well go out with someone, because in spite of what Rainbow's stars say, Les looks pretty taken with Lulu, and I'm only going to make myself miserable if I hang about in the vain hope that he's going to get tired of her.

Over lunch Rainbow whispered that she'd had a great idea.

'Porky the Paper Eater,' she said.

I looked at her, bewildered.

'We'll put Porky in Les's chalet!' she said. 'To get our own back.'

'Are you sure it was him who did the alligator?'

She nodded vehemently. 'Of course. Everyone says so. Well, who else would it be?'

'Don't know,' I said. I thought of Porky; 'He's a bit big to fit in someone's bed,' I said, 'and what about all his filling – all the cans and paper and stuff, wouldn't they all fall out?'

'Never mind,' she said. 'It'll add to the fun.'

She went off with Kevin for the afternoon later, so I was left to my own devices. Didn't want to panic Jeff by appearing by his side and being scintillating again, so I went for a walk along the beach.

Seems funny, but I've been here more than four weeks now and I've hardly seen the sea. It looked pretty much as I always remembered it, though: grey, with waves. Walked right along to the sand dunes and thought deep thoughts, mostly about James, wondering to myself where all the feelings I'd had had disappeared to . . .

Thought Porky thoughts on the way back to cheer myself up.

After supper Rainbow and I escaped from the dining room and made our way to the most convenient Porky. There are three of them, actually, but two are really prominent and under spotlights, so we had to take the one from the children's pool.

One person's arms couldn't possibly go round its fat tummy (which was stuffed with ice-cream wrappers and sticky sweet papers) and it took both of us making a huge effort to heave it off the ground and begin half-carrying it and half-rolling it towards Les's chalet. Every time a child

81

spotted us – and it was always the children, the adults seemed to see nothing strange in two Robins rolling a very large plastic pig along the ground – we stopped and pretended to be cleaning him up with a piece of tissue. We'd just reached the row of staff chalets when Rainbow gave a muffled shriek.

'Patty!' she said. 'Coming through from the nappy washing room!'

'Agghh!' was all I had time to say before Rainbow dragged me into a tiny space between two chalets and put her hand over my mouth.

We watched as Patty approached the Porky and walked all round it, looking amazed. She put out a hand and tried to push it but it wouldn't budge. 'How very strange,' we heard her mutter, and then she walked away looking at it over her shoulder as if it might run after her.

Rainbow and I watched, creased up with soundless laughter, until she'd disappeared, and then we sprang out again and heaved it towards Les's chalet, up the wooden step and through the front door – where it stuck, with me on the *indoor* side.

'Move it further in!' I said. 'Push hard!'

'I *am* pushing!' Rainbow said. 'It's his stomach. It won't go through!'

'But I'm on the wrong side,' I wailed. 'I can't get out.'

Rainbow began giggling weakly. 'Well, see you later,' she said.

I kicked at his sturdy little pink legs. 'Don't go off and leave me!' I said in a panic. 'Les'll be back any minute.'

Rainbow collapsed against the door frame, an incoherent mass of laughter. When she'd stopped wheezing and guffawing she managed to croak out: 'You'll have to climb over him, won't you?'

In the end, by pulling one of the beds close to Porky and launching myself on to his shoulders, I managed to do this. It wasn't easy, though, and Rainbow rolling around on the floor saying she'd give a hundred pounds to have a camera didn't help much, either.

We wanted to stay around to see the fun when he arrived back, but we waited half an hour or so, lurking around and dodging behind chalets whenever anyone came past, and then decided he must be out somewhere with Lulu, so we went home.

Monday, 18th August

Woke up with a start to find the sun and a large pink pig's face peering into our window.

I put out an arm and shook Rainbow. 'Wake up,' I said, 'there's a pig at the window.'

She huddled further under the blankets. 'Not first thing in the morning,' she grumbled. 'You forget I'm a vegetarian.'

A bit later, as soon as we were up and dressed, we rolled Porky back to his place by the children's pool and then presented ourselves, straight-faced, at the canteen for breakfast.

Les came up while we were in the queue. 'Morning, girls!' he said, coming up and putting an arm round each of us. 'Sleep well?'

We looked at him and he looked back at us and none of us said anything – but then he said to the chap behind the counter that he fancied a large plate of grilled *bacon*, there was nothing like a well-done slice of *porker*, and Rainbow and I scuttled away with our plates, giggling. Wonder how he got it out of the doorway, though?

Spent the day in the usual way: being utterly charming to everyone, but as it was pouring with rain most of the time and there were a lot of highly-charged children and bored people underfoot, the old charm ran a bit thin towards six o'clock.

Extra indoor activities were put on; there was a fancy hat-making competition, video horse races, free ballroom dancing lessons, a celebrity snooker match and various extra things for the children, too, but people still seemed to act as if they held Robinson's personally responsible for the weather.

'I wouldn't have come if I'd known it was going to be like *this*,' a big bossy woman said to me. She narrowed her eyes threateningly. 'I hope it's not going to *stay* like it.'

'I hope not, too,' I said cheerfully. 'Now, have you tried your luck at the video horse races?'

'I have. I lost,' she said. 'And don't suggest the hat-making competition because I wouldn't be seen dead in one.'

'Well, I'm sure it'll be fine tomorrow!' I said, moving on briskly and wondering why it was that everyone needed amusing the whole time; why couldn't they just sit quietly in a corner and keep out of trouble?

Saw Jeff just before dinner. 'Been enjoying yourself?' I asked. If he said anything about the weather I was going to thump him.

'Dave and I have been at the pool nearly all day,' he said. 'My skin's gone all wobbly.' He held out his hand as if for inspection and I touched it.

'Now I've got you,' he said, holding on to my hand tightly, 'how about coming out with me tonight?'

I pulled a regretful sort of face. 'I can't come out, actually, but I can stay on the camp with you.'

'That's good enough.' We were still holding hands and I suddenly felt really self-conscious, as if half the camp was watching – which it probably was.

'I'd better get going,' I said. 'I'll see you later.'

'Eight o'clock by the ballroom!' he shouted after me.

Had dinner and then tried, really tried, to get all enthused about going out. Gave myself a good talking-to: a girl didn't have to really fancy someone to go out with them, did she? she could just go because she enjoyed their company. Perhaps the fancying bit would come later – sort of creep up when she was least expecting it . . .

Showered and shampooed, I made my way to the ballroom, telling myself that it didn't matter that there was no little thrill of excitement when I saw him waiting there for me, it wasn't important that there was no missed heartbeat. Perhaps all that stuff was immature. Yes, that was it; perhaps I liked him in a grown-up sort of way, that's why there was no stomach-churning and butterflies.

Had a pleasant if unexciting sort of evening. He talked about football rather a lot and by the end of the night I think I could have repeated the name and position of every player in his home team. He didn't ask a thing about me, not where I came from nor *anything*, and when I tried to lighten the evening a bit by telling him about Porky he looked at me as if I was mad.

'You put a plastic pig in someone's door? Whatever for?'

'Because . . .' I creased up with laughter, 'because he put an alligator in my bed!'

It's difficult to giggle on your own, though, so we got back to talking about more interesting things: like, did I think the team manager had made a mistake by not giving Brian Someone-or-other a trial in the 'A' team, and if so, what could be done about it at this late stage?

At elevenish we walked back towards the staff chalets, me forcing myself to be agog with interest as to whether Billy Whatsit would be dropped from the team next year because the crowd didn't like him.

'We'll have to do this again,' he said outside the chalet. 'It's great talking to a girl who understands football.'

I smiled glassily and he put his arms round me. I didn't really want to, but I thought I might as well kiss him. I suppose I *could* have had a sneezing attack but I somehow didn't have the energy to. Anyway, I thought I might as well do the whole thing and see what a really grown-up and mature kiss was like.

It was – surprise, surprise – very boring. It was so boring I forgot to close my eyes, and out of the corner of them saw

Les walking back to his chalet, hands in pockets, looking gloomy.

The kiss finished (I think I only knew that because Jeff was clearing this throat ready to say something else) and over his shoulder I saw Les suddenly notice us, do a complete about-turn and begin to walk away very quickly.

'Wow!' Jeff said.

'Wow?' I echoed, taken aback.

'Some kiss, eh?'

'Some . . . er . . . kiss,' I agreed. Some kiss! I'd have had more fun kissing the door frame. 'I'd better go in,' I said. 'The friend I share with likes very early nights. She's a vegetarian.'

'Oh, right,' he said. 'See you tomorrow?'

I nodded. 'See you!'

I went in, yawning, and got ready for bed. It's going to be so *boring* being mature.

Tuesday, 19th August

'Do you think when you get older you stop fancying boys?' I asked Rainbow in bed this morning.

'Don't be daft.'

'I mean, *really* fancying them. Going all stupid and feeling sick and being unable to eat and all that business. Do you think you stop feeling like that?'

She shook her head. 'My dad died when I was ten,' she said, 'and my mum met someone else at evening classes. *She* went all silly, sitting by the phone for hours waiting for him to ring and drawing hearts on pieces of paper – all that stuff. She told me that she felt just like she had done when she was fourteen. You never get too old to feel soppy about someone.'

'Oh, good,' I said. So it's not a new, mature-type relation-ship I've got with Jeff, it's just a nothing relationship.

Sat with Michelle at breakfast and she told me she'd been to the clairvoyant on the pier the day before. 'He was wonderful,' she said, 'he really made sense. He seemed to actually know me.'

'How much?' I asked suspiciously.

'Five pounds,' she said, 'but twenty percent off for Robinson's staff. It's really worth it,' she urged, 'you'll find out so much about yourself.'

Decided that I'd go; well, I feel like treating myself and I could do with finding out a few things.

Had a quick sandwich instead of proper lunch and went out of the camp and down towards the pier, where I found Gypsy Novani between the hot-dog counter and the candy floss.

His kiosk was like a converted beach hut, and on each side of the door hung a big notice board on which were pinned letters from various celebrities I'd never heard of, all written on the same notepaper.

Dear Gypsy Novani,
   You have changed my life. I shall never be able to thank you enough!
Dear Gypsy Novani,
   A meeting with you was like a meeting with Destiny!

One just said *Marvellous! Incredible! Gripping!* like an advertisement for a film, and one was enlarged to poster size and said: *Gypsy Novani, you are a miracle man! Signed a star of stage, screen and radio who must remain anonymous!*

Read all these recommendations nervously for some moments. Was he going to change *my* life? Was I going to come out here miraculously altered, so my own mum wouldn't recognise me?

I took a deep breath and went in.

Gypsy Novani sat there eating a cheese sandwich. I knew it was cheese because there was a crumb hanging on his

lavish moustache. He wasn't dressed in robes or anything –
dead disappointing, that was – but in an ordinary old tweed
suit and open-necked shirt with dinner down the front. He
didn't even have a scarf tied round his head or an earring; in
fact, I think I could have got him under the Trades Descrip-
tions Act – he didn't look like a gypsy at all.

'Come in, my darlink,' he said throatily. 'Come in and let
us see vot the future holds for you!'

Went in and sat nervously on the edge of the stool opposite
him. He finished his cheese sandwich, chewing slowly and
looking at me steadily all the while.

I began to get jittery, or *more* jittery. 'I work at Robinson's,'
I said. 'I'm a Robin – with a red jumper, see?'

'Ah,' he said wisely.

'I've only come because . . . because . . . I mean, I haven't
got any big problems or anything, not so's you'd notice, it's
just that I wonder what's going to happen to me . . . er . . .

romance-wise and there's this boy I like ... well, I started off hating him actually but I don't now, only he's got this girl with freckles but my friend says they're not compatible so I thought ...'

'Aah!' he interrupted. He licked his lips. The crumb of cheese shook slightly but stayed where it was.

'Do you vant tarot or palm?' he asked. 'Tarot is extra.'

I wiped my hand on my skirt and pushed my palm towards him. He stared at it, twiddling bits of his moustache all the time and making knowledgeable noises. I waited, fascinated, for the piece of cheese to drop off.

'Very interesting,' he said. He put out a hand and I put my other hand in it. '*Most* interesting.'

'Er ... what is?' I asked timidly.

He dropped one hand abruptly and it banged on to the table. I retrieved it.

'You have met someone now who is going to be very, very important to you,' he said solemnly. 'You may not know it now, but he will.'

'Oh ... er ... good. Any hint who?'

'I see the initial P or D or B. Or perhaps M.'

His eyes glittered; I shifted uneasily.

'You will shortly be travelling some distance,' he said in a monotone, 'you will meet someone on this journey who will offer you something, and you should accept it. There will be much excitement and upheaval when you arrive at your destination, but you must sit tight and see things through. You must not be swayed from your goal!' he finished angrily, banging the table and making me jump.

All at once he slumped down in his chair as if he'd exhausted himself. I got my other hand back and made anguished faces at the bald spot on the top of his head. Was I supposed to go now? Leave the money and make a discreet exit?

I coughed delicately. 'May I go now?' I asked.

90

'With staff discount, four pounds,' he said. 'Recommend me to your friends.'

'Oh, I shall!' I lied. His Russian accent had all but disappeared but I didn't think I ought to mention it.

Went out and kicked stones into the sea all the way back to camp. What a con! I'd have had as much useful information if I'd gone back to Polly the fluorescent parrot. Not only that, I'd have saved £3.90.

The long journey; well, all us Robins were going home soon, he must know that. The someone who was going to offer me something, that was the man behind the counter at the station giving me my ticket – and the excitement and upheaval at my destination was Mum rushing about doing my washing and fretting because the new vests weren't out of their plastic bags. The man was useless!

Swept back into camp and found Michelle.

'I thought you said Gypsy Novani was good?' I said sternly.

She blinked at me. 'He *was*. He told me I'd be going on a long journey soon and there would be upheaval at the end of it and . . .'

'And that you'd met someone who was going to be very very important to you . . .'

'Someone whose initials were P, D, B or M!' she said. 'I wrote it all down as soon as I got out.'

What a joke. Wonder if he tells everyone the same thing? Maybe he's not really there at all. Maybe he's just a recording.

Got roped into helping out at the Fat Baby contest this afternoon, so got back to the chalet badly in need of a cup of coffee and half a dozen custard creams out of my tin.

'You're not going straight for those biscuits again, are you?' Rainbow said, looking up from some sort of big astrology chart. 'You are what you eat, you know,' she added primly.

'So a while ago you must have been a very large bar of chocolate,' I reminded her, and she shut up.

Wednesday, 20th August

'Hear you paid a visit to old Gypsy Whatever yesterday,' Les said to me outside the souvenir shop this morning.

'How did you know *that*?'

'Read it in the tealeaves,' he grinned. 'No, actually, half the girls in the camp . . .'

'Centre!'

'Centre, then, went yesterday after Michelle spread the word.'

'They needn't have bothered,' I said, 'he told me and Michelle almost exactly the same thing; all about someone whose initials were P or D or B making a big impression on our lives.'

'P, D or B, eh?' Les asked, looking at me steadily. 'Not L, then?'

'No, not L,' I said, shaking my head and trying to stare back at him without flinching. My toes all curled up one by one and my legs went wobbly, but I don't think I gave anything away.

We might have stood there forever just staring each other out, but two boys ran up dribbling a football and kicked it to Les, so of course he had to kick it back and then it developed into an impromptu game.

Walked on all of a quiver – though don't know what he's doing staring *me* out when he's all involved with the Lulu person. Bet her name's not really Lulu, anyway. Bet it's something awful like Lottie or Lena and she just calls herself Lulu because she thinks it sounds cute.

It was raining again this afternoon so they ran a bumper video of Dallas on the big TV screen in the ballroom, which made me realise with a shock that I hadn't seen TV for weeks; we never bother to watch the prehistoric black and white one in the chalet. Anything could have happened in the soap operas; I bet I never manage to catch up.

By six o'clock it was still pouring and on my way back to the chalet for a change of shoes a woman grabbed my arm and said, very nastily: 'They didn't mention *rain* in the brochures.'

Tonight the camp – centre – seemed suddenly depressing so I came back early, had a major turn-out and eventually found the sewing kit Mum said she'd put in my luggage. Removed the safety pins and pieces of sellotape from all my clothes and had a fun-packed evening doing repairs.

Rainbow was back and we were just going off to sleep when there was a banging on the chalet door. Whispered to Rainbow to ignore it.

'It's probably someone come to complain about the rain,' I said, pulling my Robin bedspread up higher.

The banging went on, though. 'Excuse me!' a woman called, 'I'm looking for my little boy.'

'It's Les's mum!' Rainbow said to me in a stage whisper.

Of course, I had to get up then, so I draped myself in the bedspread and went to the door.

A woman stood there wringing her hands. 'We went back to the chalet after the variety show and he'd disappeared. We can't find him anywhere!'

'Have you reported it to Camp Security?' I asked, pulling myself together and trying to sound calm and sensible.

'I didn't know *what* to do,' she said. 'My husband's gone to search the grounds and I knew there were some Robins in these chalets so I thought I'd come and tell you.'

'Just a moment,' I said, and I went back in, shook Rainbow's bed and told her she ought to get dressed, then pulled on jeans and a sweatshirt. 'If you go to Security, I'll go back with the mum and search the chalet properly,' I said when Rainbow was sitting up and taking notice.

Felt quite frightened walking back. What if there was a mad axe-man around?

'He's never gone out before,' the mum kept saying, 'and you hear such awful things these days . . .'

'Well, he must still be in the centre,' I told her reassuringly. 'He couldn't get past the security at the gates.'

It took half an hour to find him; he was fast asleep in the children's theatre with his head in the box that Auntie Gertie's rabbit disappears into.

'He's always had a thing about rabbits,' his mum said tearfully, as those of Robinson's staff who were awake (about half of them) sighed in relief.

Thursday, 21st August

Rainbow was up early and out collecting nettles for soup first thing this morning.

'Nettle soup is wonderfully nutritious,' she said. 'I was reading about it in the *Bean and Nut News* only yesterday. It's good for your skin and it gives you stamina and vitality and *everything*.'

She ran a bowl of water, swished the nettles around in it a bit and then looked at them doubtfully. 'I think they're going to be like spinach and disappear to nothing,' she said. 'You wouldn't be an angel and go and get me a few more stalks, would you?'

Grumbling, I pulled on my track suit. 'Where am I going to find them?'

'Everywhere!' she enthused, 'that's what's so marvellous about this sort of free food. The whole world's just one big supermarket!'

'Well, where's the counter marked "Nettles"?'

'Under the chalets, in the hedge – you've just got to open your eyes and they're there waiting for you.'

Went out, and when I came back scratching and muttering a few minutes later Rainbow remembered that she'd meant to tell me only to pick nettles with flowers on, because they didn't sting.

'Thanks a bundle,' I said, dropping a handful of bits of hedgerow into the sink. 'And what are you going to do with it all now?'

'Boil it up! It's really nourishing; I don't know why everyone's not having it.'

'We haven't got a saucepan,' I said. 'Come to that, we haven't even got an electric ring.'

She looked stumped for a moment. 'I'll put them in the kettle, then,' she said, and when I came out of the shower, still scratching nettle stings, there was a foul smell in the air and a grey-green gruel bubbling in the electric kettle.

'I thought you were joking,' I said. 'You can't make soup in there!'

'I just have,'

'But . . . it's not hygienic. All our tea and coffee will taste of nettles forever.'

But she took no notice, just kept prodding and muttering, looking like one of the three witches. Had a try of it when it was done, just to show willing, but it tasted as absolutely foul as it looked: like reheated washing-up water.

It was hot and sunny today and we all roasted in our red woollies. I think it would be a good idea if on hot days we had red t-shirts to wear; we'd still be instantly recognisable. Perhaps I'll suggest it to someone and put myself in line for a Golden Feather. None of us new Robins has ever won that, by the way. Every week it's gone to one of the long-established, one hundred per cent Robinised Robins.

The campers – guests – were very docile and well-behaved today – not much trouble at all. Most of them were so pleased to see the sun that they just stretched themselves out in long lines on the grass and sun-bathed. Hardly any of them bother to go to the beach, which seems crazy to me, but I suppose that they think as they've paid such a lot to come to Robinson's, they're jolly well going to get their money's worth and stay inside.

Saw Jeff and Dave lying in shorts beside two girls in very brief bikinis; so brief that when they turned over you got what looked like two bare bottoms staring up at you. Must say he doesn't waste much time. Wonder if his one has been treated to a shot-by-shot account of the last club away match yet?

Found a lost child and took it over to the nursery this afternoon to wait until its parents collected it. It cried all the way over there in spite of me going through my complete range of funny voices, but stopped immediately as soon as old ginger-features Lulu picked it up and spoke to it. Quite sickening, that. Wandered into nappy washing next door, just to see what it was like, and wandered out again swiftly. I hope they never get short-staffed so I have to help out in there.

Spent the evening in Robinson's Niterie showing people to their seats. Halfway through the performance a chap complained that the couple in front kept kissing and he couldn't see what was going on on stage, so I tapped the offending chap lightly on the shoulder – and nearly died two million deaths when he turned round and it was Jeff.

What I should have said was: 'Was that another Wow kiss?' but I was so taken-aback that I didn't say anything, just scuttled to the back of the theatre in confusion. I bet he thinks that I tried to split him and whoever-it-was (bare-bottom?) up because I was overcome with jealousy.

Friday, 22nd August

Helped in the souvenir shop this morning and tried to keep calm while people fought over wooden spoons, sticks of rocks and labels for suitcases with 'I've hopped to Robinson's!' on them.

Actually found time over the lunch hour to go for a swim. Thought I'd be swimming every day what with the free pools and everything, but there just never seems to be time – or there *is* time but I'm on the other side of camp and miles away from my chalet and swimsuit.

Crept in there quietly and slunk past Mike II, but I needn't have been apprehensive, he didn't even *look* at me. Mind you, he was chatting to some girl with an enormous bust and see-through yellow swimsuit, so I'm not surprised the sight of me tripping past in my faded black elasticated two-piece didn't exactly grab his attention.

Didn't much enjoy the swim, there were too many children dive-bombing and leaping, screaming, on top of me – and when one of them recognised me for a Robin and expected me to start playing porpoises, I knew it was time to disappear.

This afternoon I'd just signed a couple of autographs (a lot of the children like to collect the signatures of all the Robins) and was coming out of the funfair wondering if that was the nearest I'd ever get to being famous, when a chap called me over.

'Just the girl I need for my holiday photographs!' he said.

Pulled my jumper straight, put on beaming smile and

97

followed him round the corner – where stood the rest of his family all posed nicely in their best clothes and looking like a wedding group.

There were quite a lot of them: two grannies, an uncle, mum and dad and three children, and this dad was obviously a keen cameraman because he had the camera on a tripod and was doing the delayed shutter bit where you set the shot up, push a button, then run into a space and get in the photograph yourself.

'We just thought we'd have a genuine Robin to complete the picture,' the dad said, 'so if you'd like to stand in the middle somewhere for me . . .'

The two grannies made a space for me and I squeezed in between them. 'We've had a lovely holiday, dear,' one said, patting my hand, 'and I came third in the Glamorous Granny competition.'

The other granny stiffened and glowered at her. Rather a good glower, it was. I suppose she'd been practising it all week.

'Not quite balanced!' the dad said, still peering through the lens. We need another Robin really. Hang on a sec!'

Everyone stayed in their places – they were obviously used to being posed – while Dad disappeared round the corner into the fairground again, and came back with Les.

'Right, two Robins together in the centre!' the dad ordered. Les winked at me and made his way through.

'Now, children kneel down and you two Robins, can you put your arms round each other or something – look matey, will you?'

Smiling doggedly and staring fixedly to the front, too embarrassed to meet his eyes, I put a hand round Les's waist. His arm gripped my shoulder.

'That's better. And don't look so scared, young lady – he's not going to bite you!'

'I might!' Les said, and everyone laughed.

98

Eventually we were all looking just as the dad wanted us, so he set the trigger and rushed to stand next to his wife. We counted to ten and the camera clicked. Everyone relaxed – but Les kept his arm round me.

'Just a couple more!' the dad said. 'In case that one doesn't come out.'

Everyone in the family groaned – but I certainly didn't. I just stood there knowing that what Rainbow had said was true – you didn't grow out of feeling silly and giddy – it just depended on the person you were with.

By the third photograph I'd managed to get my mouth into gear.

'I just hope your girlfriend doesn't come round the corner in a moment and catch you here with me!' I said to Les lightly.

'I just hope your boyfriend doesn't,' he replied. '*None* of your boyfriends I should say.'

'But, I . . .'

Dad clapped his hands and the family must've all known the signal because they began to walk away.

'Let me have your address and I'll send you copies,' the dad said. 'Better still, I'll send them here.'

'That would be lovely,' I said, 'thanks.' I gave my name, said goodbye to them all, and began to walk away. Some souvenir that would be: a photograph of me with the guy who *should* have been my holiday romance. . . .

Saturday, 23rd August

We didn't have quite so many new arrivals today which was a bit sad because it means the season is coming to an end. I haven't heard definitely when my contract runs out; apparently it all depends on numbers, if we get a lot of last-minute bookings I might have to stay for the first week in September.

Had to help out in lost property this morning; last week's lot were *especially* careless, Old Jay said he had more stuff in than ever before. While I was there a woman came in saying she'd lost a set of blue underwear. Stared at her in disbelief; I mean, who goes round leaving bits of blue underwear all over camp? She eventually said she thought it had been stolen off her washing line, though.

This afternoon we had a Robins' Mini-Pentathlon for the amusement of all the incoming guests. Don't think any of them much wanted to be amused, actually, they were all too anxious to get to their chalets, get unpacked and start exploring to bother about us, but we all enjoyed it.

We did archery, running, long jump, five-a-side football and trampoline. The trampoline was the best; I'm not sure what we were supposed to have been aiming for, but I bounced up and down a lot and got out of breath and eventually bounced myself right off the side by mistake.

Les wasn't there, I think he must have been on Reception. Just as well. I expect I looked really silly: red in the face, gasping and bouncing up and down.

Have been wondering what he meant when he said *boy-friends* in that meaningful way. I've hardly had a whole series of dates since I've been here, just a few disasters. Wonder if it's serious between him and Ginger? Wonder if she lives near him at home and they'll carry on seeing each other?

Patty announced to us Robins tonight that as there was a more manageable number of guests at the moment, we'd be having a big fancy dress party for everyone the following night.

'I mean proper fancy dress,' she said, 'none of that putting a shirt on back to front, wearing a piece of cardboard round your neck and pretending you're a vicar, you've got to do something original.'

There was a general groan from everyone and a cry went up that we hadn't brought anything with us.

'Some of you will be able to borrow things from the theatre,' Patty went on soothingly. 'You'll have to see what you can have from the property department. The rest can use old sheets from the laundry, crêpe paper, or cut up things you're never going to wear again. I want you to use your imaginations!' she finished.

Rainbow, Michelle and I went back to the chalets discussing what we could be; Michelle saying she wanted to be a character in history. 'Someone very interesting and romantic: Anne Boleyn or Mary Queen of Scots,' she added.

'But they were both beheaded,' I said. 'Couldn't you find someone a bit more cheerful?'

'The Lady of Shallot . . .' Michelle mused. 'I could float across the boating pool all covered in flowers.'

'Yes, well,' Rainbow said in a business-like way. 'I shall go as a carrot.'

101

We all started laughing. 'She *said* to be original,' Rainbow said, 'and I must promote the idea of vegetarianism as much as I can.'

Don't know what I shall go as. I suppose making a very large custard-cream outfit or bar of fruit-and-nut costume is out of the question. Perhaps I'll just go as a person who's discovered, too late, that she's mad about this guy who just treats her as a friend.

Sunday, 24th August

We stuck posters up around the place this morning telling everyone about the fancy dress party, and the campers have really thrown themselves into it. Half of them seem to have brought a 'little something' in their luggage just in case of such an event – and by lunchtime I'd already seen two great big men in the First Aid post, struggling to get into nurses' uniforms that Sister had found for them.

I couldn't decide what to go as; I wanted to be funny, but also a bit glamorous. Like, I could easily have been a clown but I didn't fancy wearing the big red nose all night.

Went over to the theatre after lunch and found that half the Robins had been in before me and snazzled the best things – Emma was just walking off with a spoof Cleopatra outfit: long gold dress, beaded collar and black woolly wig, I'd really have liked that. Rummaged through what was left and found a Fairy-on-the-Christmas-Tree outfit. Robinson's is always open Christmas week and they keep the outfit for the fairy who helps give out the children's presents.

Took it into one of the dressing rooms and squeezed into it. It didn't quite give the effect I'd been after; it wasn't a dazzling Dallas-type fairy, but one who had obviously seen better days. There were thick pink tights (laddered), battered wings and a net skirt which looked as if it had been hanging in someone's sitting room window for a couple of years. I had to have it, though, because apart from a Charlie Chaplin suit and a very small policeman's outfit, it was all they had.

Carried it back to the chalet, fluffed the skirt up a bit and straightened the wire on the wings, then went up to the staff canteen to see what everyone else was going to wear.

Found Patty already there issuing instructions as to our general behaviour. Apparently we can be fairly jolly, but no jollier. ('Now, I want you to enjoy yourselves, Robins, but don't go over the top.') She handed us red rosettes to wear – even when we're in fancy dress we've got to be easily distinguishable as Robins – and said we were to circulate the whole time, not just stick with a few favourite campers. She finished by saying there was a honeymoon couple coming in that afternoon and she'd like a volunteer to look after them.

With one movement the whole of the canteen turned to look at me. I stood up and bowed.

'Well, all right, Janey can do it,' Patty said, 'but do find out first if they know each other, dear.'

Got the champagne and everything as before and went over to Reception. When the couple came in they had new clothes, matching suitcases and they showered confetti on to the floor with every movement. Even so I got their names, asked them where they were married and at what time – did everything, in fact, except ask to see their certificate. They didn't seem to notice anything odd, though – but then they were kissing each other for roughly nineteen and a half minutes of the twenty minutes I was with them, so I didn't suppose they'd have noticed if it had been Porky the Paper Eater who'd have showed them to their chalet.

The fancy dress party was a real laugh. Rainbow went as – well, I wouldn't go so far as to say a carrot, but an orange crêpe cone with a mop of green paper hair. Kevin said he'd wanted to go as a joint of beef just to keep up *his* side, but he couldn't think how to make a joint of beef outfit, so in the end he wound a sheet round him and went as a Roman.

There were loads of Romans, actually: both Roman emperors and Roman slave girls; we were knee deep in people wrapped up in Robinson's white sheets with a twirl of unspecified greenery (apparently there aren't any laurel bushes in the camp) around their heads.

Apart from them, most of the men were dressed up in women's clothes and they were the funniest of all. One man was very stout and he wore his wife's green crimplene dress; from the rear he looked reasonable – gross, but reasonable – but at the front, the hem of the dress rose right into the air where it had stretched out to cover his stomach, revealing enormous hairy legs.

Emma made a good Cleopatra and Michelle was a big teddy. She looked cute but I think she regretted it half an hour into the evening; she said being in the teddy was like being in a sauna.

Everyone had a good time. I nearly got to dance with Les, but he was in a lot of demand with the old ladies so I left him to it. Noticed that he and Ginger were both Romans; she'd twisted some gold braid round her forehead and circled her head with it. She looked really good, though it nearly kills me to write it.

Monday, 25th August

Michelle's Simon has come back for the day to see her. It was her day off today and I kept seeing them around the place hand in hand: in the pool, restaurant, sports hall and theatre. Wish *I'd* met someone and they'd come back to visit me.

Rainbow asked me today if I was going to sign up to come back Christmas week. 'I'm going to,' she said, 'and so's Kevin. He said it was really great last year, everyone was in a good mood. You don't get any grumblers at Christmas.'

I thought about it; there's a list up in the canteen and you add your name to it if you want to be considered. Went for a sneaky look at it: Les's name is down, but not Lulu's. Was tempted when I saw that, but then I thought about Mum and Dad and everyone at home; I'm sure Mum would hate me to be away at Christmas and it would mean me missing out on all the jollities there, so I haven't done anything yet.

Old Jay told me that someone had handed in a pair of false teeth today.

'A woman had the fright of her life,' he said. 'She said she was sitting in the bath and when she turned her head, there they were in the soap dish staring at her.'

Apparently someone reported them lost last week, so Jay'll be sending them on when he can decide how to wrap them.

'I don't want them to get out and bite the postman's hand,' he said.

105

Tuesday, 26th August

There was a lovely lot of mail for me at Reception today: letters from Mum, Anna, Gran *and* a big brown envelope which contained two copies of the photograph of me and Les and the departing family taken last week.

There was a note which said he'd developed the print himself and he hoped we liked it; he was quite pleased with the depth of field but wished now he'd gone up a stop with a longer exposure – whatever that meant.

Took the photograph back to the chalet, propped it up on my bedside cabinet and stared at it. I had a funny, nervous smile on my face but looked right, somehow, standing there with Les's arm round me. We'd have made a really nice couple . . .

Sighed deeply and Rainbow heard me through the bath-room wall.

'I *knew* that was a Les sort of sigh,' she said when she came out and I was still sitting there staring, 'I could tell it was.'

'What am I going to do about him?' I wailed.

She shook her head. 'I tried to tell you what the stars said but you wouldn't have it. You'll just have to hang on in there, won't you? Keep eating the sunflower seeds and hang on in there.'

This afternoon Patty spotted me in the gymnasium *not smiling*.

'Janey, love,' she said sweetly, 'it may be the end of the season to you, but to some of our guests it's just the beginning of their holiday. *Do* try to keep that smile on!'

'I'll do my best,' I said between clenched teeth, 'but some child has just dropped a bench on my foot.'

'Oh, I'm sure you'll survive!' she said jovially.

After she'd dispensed a lot of gaiety and good humour around the gym she told me that Mr Robinson, the great man himself, was expected this week.

'He hasn't been this season and he always pays us a visit,' she said.

'Oh, dear.' I curled up inwardly, imagining all the things I could do wrong. 'What's he look like?'

'That's just it,' she said, 'he's vaguely middle-aged and middle-sized and every time we see him he manages to look different. There's a photograph of him on one of last year's brochures but I can't honestly say it looks much like how I remember him.'

Got a copy of the brochure from the press office later: the photograph shows someone in a straw hat smiling a huge free-range smile, with a robin perched on his shoulder like a parrot. I bet he's the practical-joker type: all buttonholes that squirt water at you and whoopee cushions on chairs. Must keep my eyes open this week; I don't want to do anything silly.

Tried to find Les to give him his photograph but he didn't seem to be around. Think it might be his day off; wonder if it's *hers* as well?

Wednesday, 27th August

Didn't see Les at breakfast, but found him mid-morning playing football with a group of children on one of the greens. Went back to the chalet for the photograph, then when the children wandered off I went up and flourished it.

'Our group photograph!' I said. 'The man sent me two.'

'That was quick!' He took the photograph and studied it, while I studied him. Longingly.

He glanced up and almost caught me. I changed the longing look into one of polite enquiry. 'It's a nice photograph, isn't it?'

'Great!' He flung his arm round my shoulders and gave me a friendly hug; 'What a lovely couple we make!'

Instant confusion. I knew he was only joking, but considering it was just what I'd been thinking – only *meaning* it – I went as red as my jumper.

He shook me gently. 'It's OK!' he said, 'no need to get into a blind panic. I was only joking; I know you don't fancy me.'

'I . . . er . . .' I began, even more confused.

He was looking at the photograph again. 'It'll be nice to keep. Considering the number of photographs we get in, we very rarely get sent them, do we?'

'No, we don't,' I said, the redness fading to a more manageable pink.

'Well, I'll have this and . . .'

'Excuse me!' Someone tapped me on the shoulder and I turned round to see a middle-aged man beaming at me. 'I wonder if you could direct me to the beachwear boutique?'

I was just going to point him towards the shops when I suddenly remembered: *This* could be Mr Robinson! 'Certainly, sir, I'll take you there myself!' I gushed. 'Do come this way.'

Left Les standing there staring at me in amazement and not only took the chap to the beachwear boutique, but also supervised the buying of a tropical shirt depicting a sunset in violent shades of purple and orange – and it was only when he asked me if I'd like to come back to his chalet with him and help him put it on that I realised it definitely *wasn't* Mr Robinson. I smiled frostily, pointed him in direction of a big, burly man Robin and suggested that it might be more suitable if he got another man to assist him.

This afternoon Patty told all the other Robins that they were to expect a visit from the big man.

'Now, you must all think up-market,' she said worriedly.

'Remember about being a holiday centre and not a camp. Mr Robinson is most insistent that our image should change with the times so we can attract a different sort of guest; that's why he wants to get away from Knobbly Knee contests and the like.'

Reg, one of the older Robins, stood up. 'That's all very well,' he said, 'but the guests *like* knobbly knee contests. How are we supposed to persuade them that they don't?'

'By offering them alternatives, I should think,' Patty said brightly. 'More . . . er . . . restrained activities.'

'What, symphony concerts, chamber music, operas, popular stuff like that?' Reg asked, and everyone laughed.

Les stopped me on the way out. 'Now I see why you nearly fell over yourself to take that chap to the boutique,' he said. 'You thought he was old Robby.'

'Not for long,' I said, and told him what had happened.

He looked all cross and macho; quite wonderful to see, it was. 'You should have come and found me,' he said. 'I'd have sorted him out.'

Have developed an intense longing (another intense longing), this time for Mum's food. Our meal in the canteen was particularly awful tonight: mince, mashed potato with lumps, and cabbage swimming in a pale green pond. I didn't mind

109

the food here at first, being on the go all day made me so hungry I'd have eaten anything, but now I'm feeling a bit picky. Can't wait to get back to one of Mum's chicken pies or a nice chop that you might actually find a morsel of meat on.

Thursday, 28th August

People have started arriving today for the end-of-season finals of the big competitions: the Lovely Legs, Glamorous Granny, Miss Party Girl and Fat 'n' Fun.

There are ten or twelve finalists for each competition if everyone turns up. Each of these won an ordinary weekly heat and, as well as a trophy, got the offer of a free long weekend and a place in the final on Saturday.

All the staff from the managers downwards will be in to watch those, and Patty told me that if there are no other big local news items, sometimes the regional TV comes in to film the fun.

You can tell the contestants from the normal guests a mile off: all the Glamorous Grans have got three rows of pearls and blue rinses, all the Lovely Legs trip round the place in teeteringly high heels and mini skirts that look like very wide belts, the Miss Party Girls are giggly and wear dresses with sequins in the daytime and the Fat 'n' Fun – well, they're just that.

I am seeing Mr Robinsons everywhere I go; I'm even looking suspiciously at the middle-aged women in case he's decided to go the whole hog as far as disguise is concerned. This afternoon, coming out of the children's theatre, I was presented with a small box by two little girls I've got to know this week. A group of mums and dads were standing round watching and I thought this must be *it*: a practical joke from Mr Robinson: take the lid off and either the box will go up in a puff of smoke or a paper snake will leap out.

Gingerly lifted the lid: it was a sparkly brooch: red, green and blue stones in the shape of an 'R'.

'It's our goodbye present for you,' Maria, the smallest girl said. 'It's an R for Robin.'

'Pin it on! Pin it on!' Sandie said, jumping up and down. 'You do like it, don't you?'

'It's terrific,' I said, 'and it'll look lovely on my jumper.'

'I suppose we should have got your real initial,' Sandie said, 'then you could wear it when you're not being a Robin.'

'She's *always* a Robin,' Maria said indignantly.

Was very touched – also fairly relieved that they hadn't given me a 'J' in sparkly stones or I'd have felt honour-bound to wear it continuously.

There was a small riot in the gym amongst the Lovely Legs contestants this afternoon when one of them accused another one of using fake tanning lotion.

'You've got a big yellow stripe all up your calf muscle,' I heard her say accusingly. 'I can see it clear as anything.'

'That's just the light in here,' the other one retorted, 'and I'll thank you to keep your nose out of my calf muscles.'

I was just going to nervously throw myself between them but the Entertainments Manager was on hand. 'There's nothing in the rules about tanning lotions, ladies,' he said smoothly. 'You are quite free to put whatever you like on your legs.'

The two contestants glowered at each other, then both tossed their heads at the same time and began talking animatedly to people on the other side of them.

Coming back to the chalet for a quick wash and brush-up before dinner I spotted an old chap weaving across the green towards me. Thought he was drunk at first but when I looked more closely, saw that he was just very old and quavery. He was also a vicar.

'Excuse me, my dear,' he said in a trembly voice. 'Where's the church?'

111

Started giggling; it was Mr Robinson, it *had* to be.

'Is anything wrong?' he asked gently.

'No ... no.' I controlled myself, bit my lip, just in case it wasn't Mr Robinson. 'I'm ... I'm afraid the church isn't a church in the week, only on Sundays. It's the old tyme ballroom the rest of the week.'

'Oh dear,' he said.

'Some of our *guests* go to the church in town,' I said, 'that's out of the *centre*, turn left.'

He laid a shaky hand on my arm. He had one of those funny old-fashioned vicar's hats on, with the brim pulled right down so you could hardly see his face. 'Bless you, my child,' he said.

Nearly shrieked with laughter and thumped him on the back at this, but managed not to.

He tottered away towards the gate and I stood staring after him. Was he, or wasn't he? There was only one way to find out.

'Oh, excuse me, Mr Robinson!' I called.

He turned, made a 'Who, me?' gesture – and then raised his hat and waved it.

All excited – just think, I actually *hadn't* been caught out – I zipped into the canteen to see who I could find to tell. It was still early, though, and the place was deserted apart from Rainbow chatting to Kevin across the soft drinks counter.

'I've seen him!' I said. 'Mr Robinson, I mean! He's dressed as a vicar!'

Rainbow went quite pale. 'No!' she said in anguish. 'I saw him this morning – he wanted to know the way to the church and I said there wasn't one, but he might be interested in something else.'

'What something else?' Kevin asked.

She pulled a face. 'I sent him into the Lovely Legs rehearsal. I told him it would cheer him up.'

We found out later that he'd managed to trick nearly everyone – not Patty, Emma or me, though – but the entertainments manager passed the word round that he'd really enjoyed his visit and thought all this year's Robins were very charming, so *that* was all right.

Friday, 29th August

Ran into a gaggle of Glamorous Grans on my way to breakfast. They've all made friends and are going round in a pack and taking afternoon tea together, whereas the Lovely Legs are daggers drawn in high rivalry and look as if they might do each other an injury if left alone for long.

Real judges, TV stars and so on, are coming in tomorrow to judge the finals. I think it's just as well that no one from the camp is picking the winners. Safer.

I don't think I'll be here for much longer after the weekend, not unless we get loads of people rushing in tomorrow for a week's holiday. I've written to Mum telling her to air my bed, get the washing machine standing on full alert and kill the fatted calf (oops, sorry, Rainbow).

Don't know how I'll feel once I know I won't ever see Les again. It feels bad enough now, seeing him and knowing that I can't have him, but at least he's around. When he's 150 miles away and I know there's no chance of bumping into him, I think I'm going to feel terrible. Hope I don't cry all the way home and get there looking like a damp dish rag; I want to arrive all Local Girl Made Good.

It was the last heat of the Fat 'n Fun tonight; the winner misses out a bit because she doesn't get to come back for her free weekend, she's already here, of course.

All seemed to be going quite nicely as I passed through on my way to the disco, the compère was calling out the names of the entrants for them to go and parade on stage, when suddenly there was a shriek from someone in the audience.

'Cheek! I never entered! It was you who put me in for it, Sheila, wasn't it? It was you!'

The audience forgot that they were supposed to be applauding the women going up on stage and turned their attention to the disturbance: a table two rows back where a biggish woman in her twenties was hitting another woman over the head with her handbag.

Rushed over there; the one who was obviously Sheila was cowering back under the flailing handbag, not saying a word.

'You did it to spite me, didn't you, because I've got a chap this holiday and you haven't!' her friend cried.

'Just a moment,' I said, grabbing the handbag mid-swing. 'Why don't you calm down and talk about it. Maybe there's been a misunderstanding.'

'No misunderstanding!' the biggest one puffed. 'She wants to show me up in front of my chap, that's why she entered me. The cheek of it!' She snatched the handbag back. 'I'm not fat!' – here she swung it round her head – 'and as far as you're concerned I'm definitely not fun!' There was a 'whack' noise as the handbag hit its target.

I tried to get hold of it again but couldn't manage it, and in the end she had to be led off, struggling, by one of the security men.

'Honestly, fancy her taking it like that,' her friend said

114

once the contest was underway again. 'I only did it for a laugh.'

'Well,' I said, 'I don't think I'd have been *that* pleased to be entered for a Fat 'n' Fun contest, either.'

She sniffed. 'Just shows you – some people have no sense of humour.'

Saturday, 30th August

It's been like one long party here today; quite exhausting, really.

The competitions were held this afternoon and evening and most of the day I've been charging backwards and forwards between Reception, the ballroom and the theatre helping Patty and the other Robins organise things, rounding up stray grannies who weren't sure where they were supposed to be and convincing the Lovely Legs that the whole thing was only a laugh, for goodness sake, nothing to get so steamed up about.

I had a TV star judge to look after, too. Hoped it was going to be someone trendy from Channel Four but it was a hundred-year-old man, someone I'd never heard of.

A TV crew did come in, and I rushed back to the chalet and put a lot of extra eye-make-up on for the cameras in case I was needed, but when they were doing some trial shots they got a call to say there was a fire at some dockyard nearby and they were needed to film there, so off they went and were never seen again.

The finals all went quite well; even the Lovely Legs decided to behave themselves – and the winner turned out to be the girl who had (or hadn't) used the fake tanning lotion.

The Glamorous Granny final was the only one that drew a

burst of bitchiness from the other contestants, and that was because the winner was 34 and looked more like a beauty queen than a granny. She had long dark hair, was very modern – and was wearing a shocking pink flying suit while all the other contestants were in pale blue draped jersey. When the winner was declared, they all stood eyeing her up and down and clicking their false teeth. '*She's* never a granny,' one of them said, 'and even if she is she doesn't look like one. It's only us who look like grannies who should be allowed to enter.'

'I knew this would happen,' the winner said to me. 'I brought my daughter's and my granddaughter's birth certificates, just in case.'

All the winners' photographs were taken to be sent off to the national papers and they all got nice prizes – something like a suitcase or hairdryer plus cheque for two hundred pounds.

There was a big celebration afterwards with champagne and everything, but for some reason I felt much too tired to join in – and when I saw Les arrive with Lulu I just couldn't bear to stay another minute, I slipped out of the fire exit and came back to the chalet to be miserable in peace.

I could kick myself, I really could. Why didn't I realise earlier how I felt – before he got involved with *her*? I should have known all the time that when I was hating him I was only kidding myself . . .

Sunday, 31st August

It was awfully quiet on the camp today. All the contestants have gone now and we only had a small number of new campers (have given up trying to remember to call them guests) arrive yesterday. The new arrivals are all in one block of chalets, the green block, so all the other rows are completely deserted.

As soon as the people disappear all the life seems to go out of the chalets, they become just scruffy little boxes. Their curtains are already down and the decorators are inspecting them to see what's got to be done to spruce them up over the winter.

There are practically no children around; suppose they've all gone back to school, so the fairground and the children's pool are almost empty. Mike I has moved on, I don't know where, and in the amusement arcade the parrot is whistling to itself. It's all really weird – like one of those deserted film sets.

Mid-morning we had a summons to go to Patty and she told us she would only need five Robins next week – that's five of the long-term ones, of course – so all the rest of us were free to go as soon as we'd cleaned up tomorrow morning.

Felt quite devastated when she said that, even though I was expecting it. I think everyone felt the same, too; we all just looked at each other then suddenly found we'd got to rush off somewhere and be alone.

Rainbow went for a walk with Kevin – he's staying for another two weeks – and I started walking back to the chalet thinking that if anyone asked why my eyes looked funny, I'd say I was starting a cold.

Spent a while throwing bits and pieces into my suitcase and discovering things in the fluff under the bed – and then couldn't put it off a moment longer and threw myself on to the bed ready for a good old boo. One more day and I'd never see Les again!

Had just got the pillow into a nice position for thumping when there was a tap on the door. I sat up and said to come in: it was Lulu.

'I hope you don't mind,' she said, 'but I really couldn't stand it another minute.'

I swallowed hard. Couldn't stand what? Me looking at Les in a longing, unrequited-love sort of way?

'It's about Les,' she said, the pale blue eyes fixed on me intently.

'What . . . what about him?'

'Well, isn't it obvious?' she said briskly. 'He really likes you; he's liked you from the minute you got here – oh, I know he's got a funny way of showing it but some guys are like that, aren't they? You have to make exceptions for them.'

I rubbed my eyes.

'It's ridiculous – the way you're both going around absolutely daft about each other but not doing anything about it.'

'But I thought . . . you and him . . .'

She shook her head impatiently. 'It's nothing like that. We're mates – Les even knows my fiancé at home. He's been looking after me, that's all.'

'But why didn't he . . .'

'Well, every time Les went to make a move, you appeared with someone else. Then he saw you with a guy and someone said he was from home, so he thought you were going out with someone seriously; maybe even engaged or something.'

I thought fast. Someone from home? 'That – that was my brother!' I burst out.

She looked rueful. 'If only Les had known that.'

I looked at her anxiously. 'So what shall I do?'

The door crashed open and Rainbow came in. 'Look,' she said, 'I'm very sorry but I've had to do it.'

We both stared at her.

'The stars said you were right for each other but the stars sometimes need a helping hand, don't they? It was up to me to tell him before it was too late.'

'Tell who?' I gulped.

'Les! I've told him precisely what's been going on – how you've been eating your heart out for weeks and if he lets you go now he's an idiot.'

'Oh!' I clapped my hand to my mouth.

119

'It had to be said. I'm sorry if there's anything between you and him, Lulu, but . . .'

I jumped up from the bed, left them both staring after me and started running across the green towards the main camp. Halfway there I realised I didn't have any shoes on and it was raining, but that didn't seem to matter.

As I reached the fairground, Les appeared and we both stopped dead, like robots, stared at each other for a long moment and then beautifully, lovingly, straight out of Mills and Boon, we ran straight into each other's arms.

The rest of the day has been spent sorting out misunder-standings, telling each other how long we'd liked each other, when it was we'd first *realised* and other trivial and fascinating things like that.

Feel terribly light-headed and happy. I wish it had hap-pened at the beginning instead of the end of the holiday, but at least it did happen.

Monday, 1st September

I'm writing this on the train going home. This morning has been awfully gruelling, full of so many tears and hugs and kisses and promises, that I became damp dish rag-looking at eight o'clock this morning and didn't have to wait until now.

Patty said that any of us who wanted to come back Christmas week could, and seeing as Les will be here I might – but I'm going to wait and see what Mum and Dad have to say about it first.

Rainbow and I spent a good five minutes clearing up the chalet, found enough sunflower seeds to feed a lorry load of gerbils, and then she set off to catch an early train home. More tears – but we've promised to keep in touch and I'm sure we will.

Saying goodbye to Les was much worse.

'Even if you do come back for Christmas, I don't want to wait that long to see you,' he said to me on the platform just now.

'But you're miles away,' I said sadly.

'There's always weekends ... and with the money I've saved here I should be able to buy a car,' he said, giving me approximately the four hundredth kiss of the day. 'I'll be up to see you as soon as I can.'

Gave him one last hug, wiped my eyes to get rid of yet another piece of dust (don't know where it all comes from) and then got on my train.

His train is half an hour later and going in the opposite direction; he'll just be getting on it now. Feel happy and sad at the same time. Wonder if this is the Real Thing or just a holiday romance? Whatever it is, I've had a great summer ...

MARY HOOPER
Janey's Diary

Janey loves James. Often passionately. But he never seems to notice her. Janey has a dreadful brother and a mum who thinks she should wear a vest to the disco. No wonder everything goes wrong. James starts to go out with horrible Fiona, Janey's worst enemy. Can things get any worse? Will Janey ever make an impression on James – and is there life after school, beyond the cosmetics counter?

An achingly funny story of first love and romance from the author of *Janey's Summer*.

MARY HOOPER
Cassie

Cassie's one wish is to be a journalist, in a trench coat, carrying a reporter's notebook, hot on the trail . . .

So when she gets a job as a Junior on the *Weekly Echo* her dream comes true. Or does it? Making endless cups of coffee, columns of supermarket bargains. Not *another* hundredth birthday!

But then there's always Gavin, the dashing photographer from *Sixteen-on*, or Simon, who's never far away from Cassie's side . . .

MARY HOOPER

School Friends 1: First Term

The *School Friends* series tells you everything about that special first year in an all girls' secondary school, as told by Mickey.

'When I first went to Park Wood, I thought it was going to be rotten and boring and stuffy. Well, Mrs Mackie wasn't exactly a laugh a minute, but what with sausage inspection, keeping Alison down, spotting dangerous criminals, trying to keep the twins from killing each other, discovering the dark secret of the poison cupboard and being Mistress of Ceremonies for the end of term Revue, there wasn't a lot of time to get bored ... and then of course there were the other girls ...'

The sequels to *First Term*, *Star*, *Park Wood on Ice* and *The Boys Next Door* are also available from Mammoth.

MARY HOOPER
School Friends 2: Star

The *School Friends* series tells you everything about that special first year in an all girls' secondary school, as told by Mickey.

'Fleur thought Araminta Eversage sounded like a herb shampoo. But she was a girl and she'd come from drama school especially to cause havoc in Mrs Mackie's class. Well, when she and Cerise weren't staring out of the window at the boys or discussing lipsticks, they were rehearsing Araminta's famous cat food advertisement. And then the camera team came to school . . .'

Star is the sequel to *First Term. Park Wood on Ice* and *The Boys Next Door*, books 3 and 4 in the 'School Friends' series, are also available from Mammoth.

A selected list of titles available from Teens

While every effort is made to keep prices low, it is sometimes necessary to increase prices at short notice. Mandarin Paperbacks reserves the right to show new retail prices on covers which may differ from those previously advertised in the text or elsewhere.

The prices shown below were correct at the time of going to press.

☐	7497 0095 5	**Among Friends**	Caroline B Cooney £2.99
☐	7497 0145 5	**Through the Nightsea Wall**	Otto Coontz £2.99
☐	7497 0582 5	**The Promise**	Monica Hughes £2.99
☐	7497 0171 4	**One Step Beyond**	Pete Johnson £2.50
☐	7497 0281 8	**The Homeward Bounders**	Diana Wynne Jones £2.99
☐	7497 0312 1	**The Changeover**	Margaret Mahy £2.99
☐	7497 0473 X	**Shellshock**	Anthony Masters £2.99
☐	7497 0323 7	**Silver**	Norma Fox Mazer £3.50
☐	7497 0325 3	**The Girl of his Dreams**	Harry Mazer £2.99
☐	7497 0280 X	**Beyond the Labyrinth**	Gillian Rubinstein £2.50
☐	7497 0558 2	**Frankie's Story**	Catherine Sefton £2.50
☐	7497 0009 2	**Secret Diary of Adrian Mole**	Sue Townsend £2.99
☐	7497 0333 4	**Plague 99**	Jean Ure £2.99
☐	7497 0147 1	**A Walk on the Wild Side**	Robert Westall £2.99

All these books are available at your bookshop or newsagent, or can be ordered direct from the publisher. Just tick the titles you want and fill in the form below.

Mandarin Paperbacks, Cash Sales Department, PO Box 11, Falmouth, Cornwall TR10 9EN.

Please send cheque or postal order, no currency, for purchase price quoted and allow the following for postage and packing:

UK including BFPO	£1.00 for the first book, 50p for the second and 30p for each additional book ordered to a maximum charge of £3.00.
Overseas including Eire	£2 for the first book, £1.00 for the second and 50p for each additional book thereafter.

NAME (Block letters) ....

ADDRESS ....

....

☐ I enclose my remittance for ....

☐ I wish to pay by Access/Visa Card Number ☐☐☐☐☐☐☐☐☐☐☐☐☐☐☐☐

Expiry Date ☐☐☐☐